# GLASS
# BOTTLES

# GLASS BOTTLES

A Fiction Novella

By

## J L GOODWIN

~DEDICATED IN MEMORY OF
LEONE MAE~

Cover art by Linda Martin, and acknowledgement to the writers of the ballad "The Air That I Breathe", Albert Hammond and Mike Hazelwood.

# ONE

The polo match was winding to its close with a score that seemed too uneven to be changed by any standard of miracles.

"Papa, I must go to the shade. The sun is too much."

Jessica stood from the seating arrangement at the northern end of the field. Her father nodded approval and motioned towards the row of giant cottonwoods. Horses and carriages had been drawn along the tree's shadow line and blankets laid upon the grass, providing a cool refuge for spectators. Arnold Goodwin was an imposing figure of a man; stern, hard features, quite tall and thickly bearded, yet tailored immaculately.

She felt a little less flushed as she leaned against a towering tree trunk and smoothed her dress. It was soaked in perspiration. In her view corsets were an inconvenient hindrance that served no purpose except to increase one's feelings of limitation and confinement.

1

"Hello. May I offer my handkerchief?"

Jessica was startled back to the moment. A gentleman stood before her in shirtsleeves. He bent toward her spreading his jacket at the base of the tree.

"My name is Federico Fernando De Silva. Please sit here if you wish."

Jessica stretched out an ungloved hand as her father approached.

"Jessica, we will be leaving now."

She turned and took his arm, but not before glancing toward the gentleman's dark brown eyes. As father and daughter walked towards their carriage, the handsome stranger addressed a man who was standing nearby.

"Armister find out who that young woman is before we leave for Venice."

Later, on that July evening in 1885, no one in the Goodwin family household seemed to notice that Jessica had removed her corset.

"Jessica, did you know that fellow, the one who was engaging you in conversation? It is not proper to accept a handkerchief from a stranger. It is not correct under any circumstances, most especially if you are not being supervised."

Jessica was sitting at the dining room table, wishing to be no-where.

"Yes Papa, I respect what you are saying. I seem to have almost fainted in the heat of the day. For a moment I was not aware of my surroundings."

She reached for a sip of mint julep and settled back in the chair.

"It won't happen again, Papa. I think it best that I wait until the weather cools before I attend another polo match."

"Very well, Jessica. I admit that since your mother's passing last year, I have been at a loss assisting you in the simplest of social skill development."

After a long pause Arnold Goodwin continued.

"Your mother's sister Olivia lives in New York City. I know you haven't seen her since you were a small child, but do you remember her?"

"Yes Papa, I do remember Auntie Olivia. I loved her smile and her happy frame of mind."

"Very well then. I am considering sending you away for an extended period, to Olivia's home in New York. Literature has always been a great talent of yours and this will prepare you to take another step in your cultivation as an educated and socially graceful woman of today's times. You are the only child from my marriage to your mother and I strongly feel that it is time for you to be privy to the guidance of a mature woman."

Jessica rose from the table.

"Papa, I am very tired after today's event in such difficult heat. I need to retire now and appreciate your concern for my well being. Perhaps visiting Auntie Olivia and discussing this with her would be the thing to do. I would be dreadfully unhappy if for one moment we were imposing upon her in any way."

When Jessica had removed her constraining corset she failed to notice that her firm young breasts were spilling over the bodice of her dress. She was also unaware that the servants had noticed. Arnold Goodwin could not help but see his beautiful daughter's ripening womanhood. As he retreated to the library Arnold poured himself three fingers of brandy from the glass bottle.

The horse drawn coach ride from Baltimore to New York City was bumpy, long and exhausting. Jessica's thoughts drifted to her New York City destination and the reunion with Aunt Olivia, and then toward the lady passenger sitting at her left. The young woman sat still ... then bounced, as each rut in the road seemed to steal another breath from her body. She tugged at her corset occasionally, with an expression of great angst. The two male passengers occupying the opposite seat had dozed off to sleep, a feat that seemed remarkable to Jessica. She turned to face the young woman sitting beside her.

"My name is Jessica."

"I am Amanda. Thank you for speaking to me. I am so terribly uncomfortable. I just cannot breathe. Do you know when we will stop to water the horses?"

"I do not know the schedule for this coach, but I do know that we have been travelling for several hours and we must stop soon. These poor horses are sweating so much that I can smell them here inside the coach. Besides, Amanda, it looks to me like you could use a drink of cool water right now."

Amanda gave a deep sigh and a tear rolled down her cheek. With head bent forward Jessica teetered to her feet.

"Well, enough of this!"

She banged the heel of her shoe against the driver's side of the coach, her voice raised to the point of screaming.

"Stop this coach right now!"

No further direction to the drivers was needed. The horses quickly responded to the pull of the reins and the wheels slowed to a stop. A dusty, well muscled man appeared at the coach door.

"Madame, is there a problem?"

Jessica raised her voice once again as she yelled.

"Open this door immediately and let me and my fellow passengers feel the solid Earth under our feet."

The driver pulled open the door of the coach with ease and Jessica stepped down, with Amanda's hand clasped firmly in hers.

"My friend and I are going to take a rest under that tree and when we return I want two cups of the barreled water sitting on these seats. If we are not near a watering hole for these precious horses, then I strongly suggest that you give them barrel water before we set off again."

The two male passengers remained inside, staring at each other with open mouths as the scene unfolded before them. Jessica gently pulled Amanda behind a group of evergreen trees, into a refreshing cool breeze.

"Amanda." Jessica's voice was almost a whisper. "I will unbutton the back of your dress. You can take off your corset and place it near the trunk of one of these trees. I will re-button your dress and leave it loose enough for you to breathe with comfort."

Jessica smiled. The sound of water being poured was clearly audible.


"Oh, Jessica, you are so beautiful. I have no words. You are as lovely as your mother, my dear sister Sarah. Come in. Please come in."

Olivia's ability to nurture was certainly coming from a high place close to her soul. She had no children of her own. That, however, was merely a biological fact and bore no relationship to her loving, accepting nature.

Over the course of the months that followed, Jessica learned why Aunt Olivia had not played a larger role in the family. When Sarah married Arnold Goodwin, Sarah's side of the family was firmly put in their place. Arnold Goodwin lived for his ideals of a southern gentleman's presentation in life and had little, if any, room for a family of Yankee origin. Olivia did disclose to Jessica that she was very surprised that Arnold had arranged for his daughter to travel to New York City and be exposed to a Yankee point of view.

Many mixed feelings regarding her southern heritage and her new found liberty played on Jessica's mind as the months in New York City became one year. Her aunt's unconditional love and tolerant outlook provided a sanctuary of quiet peace. Jessica became deeply engrossed in her studies of English literature and the experience of freedom in the expansion of her true nature. Hours of delightful sharing and laughter echoed through Olivia's pristine apartment in the Bronx ward of New York City.

On one particularly quiet evening Jessica was at home studying her lessons, while her aunt attended an opera at Townsend Theatre. There was a knock at the apartment door. Jessica pushed her chair back from the desk. There was another knock as she reached toward the door. A familiar figure stood under the shadows of the porch lantern.

"Hello Jessica, my name is Federico De Silva. Do you remember? We met at the Baltimore polo match last year."

Jessica was not quite sure how she should respond to the unexpected gentleman caller. To her relief, within moments, Aunt Olivia arrived and began climbing the seven brick steps to the porch landing. Olivia paused, and stared up into the sable brown eyes of Federico de Silva.

"Oh Jessica dear, please feel free to invite your gentleman caller into our parlor for a nip of spirits. The opera was lovely and I would so appreciate your company and his. Do introduce us."

"Auntie Olivia, this is Mr. Federico De Silva. We made acquaintance at a polo match in Baltimore, Maryland."

Olivia smiled and took Federico's arm as they followed Jessica into the parlor. Federico spoke as they entered the room.

"Ladies, may my first mate Armister De Angelo join us? He is standing at the street lantern."

"Oh, by all means Mr. De Silva. Miss Jessica and I would be most honored."

Armister was summoned inside and politely removed his hat.

# Two

Fernando Welsh was born in Phoenix, Arizona, on September 4th, 2010. Anna Maria Russo had married Henry Kevin Welsh on the eve of Fernando's birth. A Justice of the Peace in Maricopa County facilitated the quick formality of vows as he stared at the size of the young woman. Anna Maria was Catholic and had arrived straight from Sicily. She was what had been referred to in earlier years as a 'mail order bride'. Henry was slurring the vows and attempting to stand erect.

"Mr.... Mr. Welsh. Are you intoxicated? If so, I am bound by law to not give the marriage vows."

"I am one hundred percent sober."

Despite knowing full well that Mr. Welsh was not in a sober frame of mind, the Justice pronounced the two 'husband and wife'.

The following morning baby Welsh made his arrival. He opened his huge sable brown eyes and looked at Anna

Maria. She took a deep breath and whispered to her son. "I will never forget your beautiful father. His eyes are yours. Though he is dead, his Mediterranean blood will flow in your veins forever. I name you Fernando."

"Jessi, you will be late for your appointment." A cheery voice trilled through the apartment digital intercom. Jessica's mother was considered to be a very 'all together' mom. That was the lingo used by friends to describe her when she had given birth to Jessi on a mild December night, twenty-two years earlier. Firmly committed to single parenthood, Lauren Englund had been as studied and organized for the event as any woman of her generation could be.

From the first signs of labor Lauren monitored each contraction by the clock, carefully entering the time, duration and intensity of each one. In between the spasms she walked back and forth in the modest New York City flat, glancing down to the street below as giant snowflakes began to drift past the bay window and fall silently onto the sidewalk two stories below. Jessica Lynn Englund arrived in that Greenwich apartment at 4:00 AM on December 4th, 2011. An experienced nurse practitioner assisted her entry into the world.

With the exception of disturbing dreams prior to Jessi's birth, the pregnancy had been a period of peace and contentment. The same dream had returned on four separate nights: a steep cliff, its upper part covered with a dense black fog that obscured the skyline. High waves crashed against the rocks below, where two glass bottles glistened, wedged firmly between the boulders. Lauren seemed to be observing this dream scene from a small island off shore. With unbearably cold rain pounding her face, she strained to see through the mist. The whispers heard high above the crashing waves and biting winds were haunting. Lauren shivered at the recollection. Each time the dream occurred she had awakened at 4:00 AM.

"Hey, Nando, I'm gonna race you home."

"With my long legs, Justin? You gotta be kidding'"

The race finished with Fernando Welsh waiting for his brother on the front porch of their South Phoenix Arizona home. Justin approached out of breath. Nando slapped him on the back, making breathing even harder.

"Leave me alone ass hole!"

"Aw lil bro, you want me to leave you alone, huh?"

The skirmish ended when Henry Welsh drove into the modest driveway.

"Hey, you guys, clean up this mess right now!" Henry yelled as he stomped up the stairs to the front door.

"Justin." Fernando whispered. "Let's clean the yard up and see if the firemen will let us hang out over there like they did last week."

By July 2026 Phoenix had broken all previous heat records. Planetary warming reached what would be its peak before stabilizing during the next decade. The metropolitan area had a loss of population as thousands of people per year sought to live in less harsh climates. Nando spun around, drenched by an unexpected rush of cool water. His lips tasted like sea salt. For a second, he felt that he'd been hit by an ocean wave. Justin laughed and gave Nando another hit from the garden hose.

⁓

Jessica eased aboard the people mover transport and found only an aisle seat open. Although it was only a short ride to her dentist's office, she would have preferred a window seat. Smiling while remembering how the nuns at Holy Cross Academics decided that her desk could no longer be near the window, Jessica could still hear Mother Mary Martha's high squeaky voice.

"Jessica, meditation is for chapel time, not academic time!"

Closing her eyes, Jessica surveyed her inner world quietly. After completing undergraduate studies at the Long Island campus of NYU, the time had come to consider a master's degree selection. She took a deep breath in an attempt to shake the uneasiness that would frequently steal into her consciousness, an uneasiness that always led to feelings of melancholy. Making a mental note to find a neurologist who would do a brain-mapping scan to find out if there was any organic reason for these moments of sadness, Jessica dismissed the thought. The episodes of melancholy had begun with the onset of puberty. Her mother Lauren felt it was a hormonal issue and over the course of those years had arranged examinations by several endocrinologists. With the exception of low serum blood levels of monoamines and serotonin, all of the diagnostic test results were within the normal range for her age. Jessica was smoking medical grade marijuana but found her attention span becoming shorter. This had made her last few months at the university increasingly difficult.

The people mover slowed to a halt at Jessica's destination. It was a quick indoor-tube ride to the 56th floor and before the thoughts of melancholy had entirely passed, Jessica found herself seated in front of Dr Halisina.

"Oh Jessi, the tar stains on your teeth are going to take Gia at least fifteen minutes to clean off."

Jessi leaned back into the horizontal chair. There was that relentless internal tug to release the present environment and to float to some space of comfort with no bounds. Jessi dove inward and mentally let go of all need to control the buzzing of ultrasonic instruments. With that easing… the whining noise became silent.

Free for the rest of the day, it seemed to be an ideal opportunity to take a walk and contemplate. She considered riding the people mover to the shipyard area down by the harbor. The March air was crisp but spring had arrived in New York City, the mildness of the breeze swirled about with a promise of flowers and birds soon to come. The way to the pier led past the row of familiar shops that had delighted her as a child. One in particular, a curio shop selling old nautical decorum, had always invoked a strange fascination. She stared awhile into the fog-smeared window before entering. The small interior was wet with sea mist that had probably never dried out. Its swollen wooden panels and shelves gave off an aroma of once-living trees that knew not that they had been cut dead.

The first item to catch her eye was a model of an old schooner, mounted within a glass bottle. Its fully raised sails seemed to be animated by an invisible wind.

"Could you tell me the price of this model?"

Wherever Jessi travelled people were affected by her serene beauty and, as a consequence, they found themselves talking about things they normally would not have shared. So it was that day, in the small shop at the pier.

"This model was made at the beginning of the twentieth century. It was designed after a schooner owned by a man named Federico De Silva in the late 1800's.

He named the vessel 'Liberty'. De Silva was a shipping magnate. This model of his private schooner is priced at $2,200. My grandfather was running the business when a man brought it in. He bartered with my grandfather."

Jessi was deep in meditation. It wasn't unusual for the sea air to lift her high in consciousness. Today she found herself barely able to stay grounded long enough to converse with this gentleman who was apparently the current shopkeeper.

"I'll take the model ... Mr.?"

"Call me Stan, Miss. I am the shop owner".

A few minutes later Jessi found herself carrying a bundled treasure. Any practical reason for the purchase was cognitively out of her reach. She made her way home, uplifted by the anticipation of adventure.

⌣

By 2020 foreign terrorism was generally contained outside the borders of the US. There had been the devastating use of chemical weapons by foreign terrorists several years before. A major international terrorist organization network acknowledged culpability for the saran gas that was loosed into the ventilation systems of a major US airport. Simultaneously, the terrorists had released the gas into one of the country's largest interior shopping malls. Within days following the disaster there was a near collapse of the US economy. However, New York City was spared the chemical assaults.

Within three months of the attacks the value of the US dollar dropped 15%. The Dow Jones Industrial Average plummeted. In 2024, when Jessi was thirteen, her mother Lauren, a public defender for the City of New York, married. There was no denying that her lifestyle was dramatically changed by Lauren's decision to marry Charles Warren.

Charles Warren was the chief administrator of Grace Hospital in New York City. There would be no future financial concerns for Lauren, or her daughter. In 2033 they were living in a large apartment in Manhattan. Here Jessica had ample room to develop the soul searching that seemed to be her calling. She would spend hours reading romance novels, yet she rarely dated. During periods of depression she would isolate herself, emerging only to walk in Central Park. Walking, regardless of the weather, much to the concern of her mother, Jessi preferred storms to sunshine. Her periods of melancholy were also a frequent worry. Both Charles and Lauren were amazed when she graduated from NYU two semesters earlier than the average student.

On the evening of March 4th, 2033, Jessi carried her precious bottle gently as the doorman escorted her up the tube to the forty-first floor of the twice remodeled Skyscape Towers.

# GLASS BOTTLES

Charles Warren had a keen eye for fine art. When Jessi showed him the schooner model contained within the glass bottle, he remarked at the stunning detail and carried it carefully to his study. There he examined the delicate woodcarving and intricate, starched muslin sails.

"Jess, this is a very fine piece. It seems like one could actually hoist these sails. The design is immaculate!"

Jessi leaned closer as Charles studied the schooner.

"Jess, pull up a chair and use this magnification lens to see the remarkable detail."

The sun had set. Flickering logs in the marble fireplace danced their light throughout the study, increasing the sense of mystery that surrounded their shared discoveries.

"Dad, what does that inscription say? Right there, on the fore of the hull."

Charles read the tiny inscription.

"Liberty My Jessica".

Nando pulled on his gear as the alarm at headquarters sounded. The avalanche had been predicted. No one knew just when the shelf of snow on the remaining tip of Mt Rainier would crumble. Mt Rainier had begun dripping vast quantities of melting ice each year. Although hikers were warned to stay away from the mountain, the search and rescue teams of 'Sea-Tac S&R' were kept busy all summer long. The crew viewed headquarters on the monitor as the captain of S&R appeared.

"There are four hikers buried beneath the avalanche. We have satellite phone communications with three of them. Map coordinates will now be shown. Bring them home."

Nando and Justin were at the base of Rainier in five minutes. The mountain was lit with laser signals coming from the indicated depth of ten to twenty feet.

"Nando, base will be here with equipment in ten minutes."

Four crew members had arrived from Avel-Man, a private rescue company.

"I count three signals with a slight pulsation from the second ridge, just above the timber line."

Nando was using his laser detector and began the ascent. The snow was slushy at the base. The further he climbed, the firmer the snow became. The weak laser signal disappeared from his scanner. He continued climbing towards the last recorded beam. Snow crumbled beneath his boots and propelled him back twenty feet.

"Hey, Nando. 87 here. Wait for equipment."

"That would be a roger ... but we are going to lose the signal for this one. It's off my scope now. Going higher."

The snow did not seem cold. The sun was as bright as the Phoenix summers that Nando remembered so well.

He looked from the corner of his eye and saw Justin moving up on his right.

"Hey, little Bro'."

"I got 'em back on signal, big Bro'."

Together, they completed the rescue.

In 2034 IGID (International Genetic Information Data) was the online data base for billions of people worldwide. The bank provided data regarding lineage history as well as complete extended family information. Depending on the researcher's skill and patience, data such as extended family constellations could be retrieved. Many personal history records could be viewed through complex coded databases. Even genetic mapping and complete background checks were available online after US civil right amendments were modified. Genetic history was sketchy for persons born before DNA mapping became required at birth.

That spring Jessi spent all her free time researching the name Federico Fernando de Silva, the owner of the schooner 'Liberty' and its inscription 'My Jessica'. There was a record of his birth in 1855 in Rome, Italy. It was quite evident that Federico De Silva had numerous places of residence during his lifetime and in a search of recorded business documents, his name appeared 72 times.

The name of his shipping company was first re-corded as 'De Silva de Rome', but was changed in 1900 to 'Europa'. There was neither record of his marriage nor record of death.

Adversely though, springtime was delivering its usu-al melancholy for Jessi, and Lauren encouraged her to resume psychiatric therapy.

"But Mom, maybe this depression is organic and not psychological. There is nothing in my life that has been traumatic. I should have a brain map done. You and Dad have provided me with all the emotional and physical support that anyone could possibly have."

Jessi was smiling an impish grin that assured Lauren that there was still plenty of fire in her being.

"Okay, Jess, talk to your Dad about any new tests that are available in neurology and I won't bother you about seeing your psychiatrist."

Lauren felt a slight ache as she left Jessi at her com-puter and returned to talk with Charles in the study.

"Come in, Darling."

Charles leaned back in the soft plush chair that had begun to conform to his body shape.

"I know you too well Lauren. You are concerned about Jessi again."

Charles was a distinguished-looking man. He was handsome in a rare way, a way which spoke of strong char-acter. His persona was intense, yet kind. Lauren leaned to kiss Charles lightly. There were tears in her eyes.

"Jess is fine, Lauren. It's her nature to be as she is. These periods of sadness are her way of finding herself. If we come across as being concerned about her isolative behaviors it will seem as if we don't accept her as she is. Haven't we learned that trying to change someone causes them to suffer far more than they would if we just stand near and love them?"

Lauren stared out of the window to the city lights.

"You are right as always when it comes to Jess. The way that you love her is constant. It gives me hope that all is well."

Smiling through the tears, she cuddled her body into the chair with Charles. He stroked her soft brown hair as he spoke.

"And I almost forgot to tell you that Jess and I have been talking quite a bit lately. She is sharing her feelings with me more. In fact, just last week she was telling me about a dream that she's having, one that is repeating. I am sure it has to do with her work in researching the owner of that shipping firm, that man who had his schooner miniaturized in a bottle. But never the less, she is excited that, in her dream, there are two glass bottles stuck in the rocks on a stormy sea cliff."

As autumn approached, Jessi chose the discipline of European History for her postgraduate studies at NYU. The first semester included classes on the ancient Roman Empire, sure to keep her deeply involved in study. By mid October she was planning the outline for her thesis.

It would be based on the organization and growth of the European shipping industry.

"May I sit with you, Jessi?"

As Alden Lucci approached the table, he was balancing a caff-hit drink and a plate of fries on his solar-tronic notebook. All the while a trail of paper napkins fell to the floor in his wake. Jessi looked up and smiled at Alden, glancing at the trail of white paper that formed a path to the table.

"Sure, Alden."

The dining hall at NYU was completely automated but the ambiance was warmed by student chatter and the soft clicking of notebooks. Jessi's smile was graciously accepted by Alden. He knew that conversation wasn't necessary and he also knew, from joining Jessi during other dining hall meals, that she would soon resume reading and he could stare at her physical loveliness without being noticed.

Alden was not aware that Jessi had developed telepathic skills. In 2033 the philosophy of one universal mind had been considered scientific fact, though few of the populous understood the concept or had developed the skill to utilize that fact. Making the knowledge useful or practical in individual life experiences was still not the norm.

As Alden's eyes roamed every viewable inch of Jessi's body, she saw him retrieve memory of her strolling across the NYU campus and then saw his image of her naked, walking towards him in the rain. Inwardly Jessi smiled again as she noticed that Alden didn't quite have her breasts visualized correctly.

December came to New York City bearing nor'easter ice storms with wind and sub-zero temperatures. The routes of the enclosed people movers, subways, and cabs (now referred to as private escort) remained fully operational but most university students were working online from their homes.

Lauren was relieved that Jessica had found such an absorbing interest in her postgraduate studies. Jessi had not shared the story of the repeating dreams with her Mom. However, hardly a day passed when Lauren did not ponder upon what Charles had shared with her regarding Jessi's disclosure to him.

She stood in front of the fireplace mantel in Charles' study. The schooner model of 'Liberty My Jessica', set with sails erect, enclosed in the tightly corked glass bottle, filled with light from the blazing flames. Her thoughts drifted back to 2011, to when she had been pregnant with Jessi. A shiver ran through her as she recalled the haunting dreams of ice cold waves crashing against the sea cliffs, of squinting through the rainy mist and seeing the two glistening glass bottles trapped tightly between the rocks.

But now December 4th was approaching. In two days' time Jessica Englund Warren would turn twenty-three. It was time to read through the menu options for the small gathering she was arranging.

Skyscape Towers provided a gourmet catering service that was available by reservation for its residents. Lauren had invited two of her daughter's friends to join the birthday dinner party. Kaylyn had been a close family friend since she and Jess attended Holy Cross Academics, from elementary through high school. Kaylyn's mother, Irene, worked for the public defender's office when Lauren had been an attorney there. It always amazed Lauren and Irene how very different Jess and Kaylyn were, personality wise, yet they were such loyal friends.

Kaylyn arrived with her hair styled in the latest spiked fad, bearing sections of colors true to the Italian flag. From her left to right, green, white and red gel tufted spikes framed her finely chiseled facial features. It was difficult to imagine how big a smile her tiny face could break into. But it always did. Kaylyn danced into the foyer of the apartment, grinning from ear to ear as she presented Jessi with a birthday package wrapped in green, white and red synthetic.

Alden Lucci had been the first guest to arrive and was becoming more sociable after his second glass of Iglesias Red Merlot, circa 2010. He was doing a superb job of not spilling any food and seemed to know that two glasses of wine would be his limit.

Following a meal of pasta basil marinara with endive salad followed by a pecan tort with pineapple glaze, the birthday party moved into the grand room where Jessi's gifts were placed. Charles had built a magnificent fire in the largest of the apartment's marble fireplaces. Lauren poured tiny pony glasses of crème de cocoa for the guests to sip. Jessi had placed the schooner model upon the grand room mantel. The flames from the giant fire reflected brilliantly as they seemed to lick the sails of the schooner set snugly within the glass bottle.

Kaylyn's gift had brought tears to Jessi's eyes. Now the bold flag of Italy could be added to her collection of European flags. Alden had been anxious for Jessi to open his gift to her. After changing the position of his crossed legs numerous times and following several nervous coughs, he requested another glass of crème de cocoa and was finally still. Everyone's focus was on the package that he had brought. The outer box identified the contents as being manufactured by RIZO Electronics. Within was the software program for immediate access to real time video stream of the Lunar Colony. Alden could no longer contain his excitement.

"My Dad has been at the colony for six months now. He's a geologist and an engineer for NASA's lunar operation LUNA IV. He sent me two sets of software. I wanted Jessi to have one."

Alden seemed very proud of himself. Jessi accepted the generous gift graciously, but suddenly felt strangely warm and flushed. As she stood to give Alden a hug there was a loud popping noise, then the sound of shattering glass. Splintered shrouds covered the fireplace hearth. The schooner model lay ablaze in front of the logs. Charles jumped to his feet, but the sails of the ship had ignited instantly. In a matter of seconds the old wooden carving was almost destroyed. One of the masts crumbled into powder as Charles wrapped the flaming remains in a towel.

"Dad, I want the schooner mounted within a hermetically sealed clear case, just as it is now."

The atmosphere was somber on the morning following Jessi's birthday celebration. Charles and Lauren sat with their daughter, sharing brunch.

"Oh, Jessi, are you sure you want to look at the ship all burnt and broken?" Lauren was tense.

"Yes, Mom. I want it exactly as it is. I am not sure why, but I am very certain."

Within two weeks the charred hull of the model, plus every bit of retrievable glass and ash was mounted in a clear acrylic case. The artist at Antiqua Preservation & Restoration was fascinated with the remaining detail of carving on the schooner.

"We tried very hard to mount the remains in a way that would show its strength. There is a sense of determination connected to this piece of art. All of us here have marveled at it. Look. One can still read 'My Jessica' ... inscribed, right here."

It was Christmas Eve. Snow fell softly like a lacy scarf across the city streets. Jessi felt a warm glow as she once again carried her treasure home.

"Jessi, why don't you ask Alden to help you download the language software? He just got his PhD in geekness and I'm sure he would be delighted!"

Kaylyn was stretched across Jessi's bed, sipping a protein drink. Jessi frowned at the computer monitor.

"Well, Kaylyn, reason number one, he undresses me in his mind every time we see each other. Reason number two is that his dad is home after eight months at the lunar colony so he'll want to spend all his free time with him. Reason number three is how can I ask him to download this language translator software when I haven't even downloaded the LUNA IV software he gave me?"

Kaylyn jumped to her feet.

"Let's put that LUNA feed stuff in. It'll be a breeze to download compared to this language program. Then if you still can't figure out the program, at least Alden will know that you cared enough about the gift that he gave you for your B-Day."

Jessi managed a nod of her head and they prepared the LUNA chip for download. There was a complex code and key system required to begin operations, but the tutorial walked them through the process in minutes. The required numerous apps completed the download.

"Wooha! Scope it out Jess!"

Kaylyn nearly pushed Jessi out of her chair. The images were crystal clear. Within a few moments both had mastered the zoom control and were watching the facial expressions of Earth aliens on the moon. Through what appeared to be a smaller environmental helmet than they expected to see, they watched a masculine face smile and excitedly read his moving lips.

"That's an affirmative, six nine. Going to Y seven. Over."

"Girl, that is so awesome!" Both young women were mesmerized.

"This is unbelievable!"

Kaylyn raced to the bathroom and, in her excitement, got there just in time. As Jessi called on the intercom for her dad to join the viewing, Lauren reached the top of the stairs wondering what all of the ruckus was about.

Charles ran the tutorial on partial screen and found the code for channel changing. To everyone's amazement, they began viewing the inside of an environmentally controlled building. Men and women were engaged in projects that varied from sitting before communication equipment to serving meals. The audio feed was excellent when the zoom microphone was used.

# GLASS BOTTLES

That evening in early February 2035, four space groupies spent the night in Jessi's room visiting the moon.

⌒

Alden stepped into the entrance of his parent's east side apartment. Walter Lucci greeted his son with a warm hug.

"How do you like NASA's new LUNA V uniform?"

"Hey Pops, you look so good!"

Walter's smile was infinite.

"Son, I'll be fine as usual and home before Christmas. And I intend to video phone you every week."

"Pops, Jessi has a favor."

"What does that beautiful woman want of this humble old man, may I ask?"

Walter always smiled when the topic was about Jessi. Alden couldn't miss the light that swept across his father's eyes at the mere mention of her name.

"Pops, the package doesn't weigh much so it shouldn't be a problem to transport. Jessi wants the package buried in the lunar crater Italiano. Here are the longitude and latitude calculations."

"What's in the package son?"

"It's the hull of a burned out schooner model made in 1900 or so. It's all encased in acrylic and is hermetically sealed."

Walter was pensive for a moment.

"You know it must be put through the de-contamination series, and of course it will be thoroughly radiated."

"It won't hurt it, Pops."

"Well ... it's as good as done.  I'll video phone you when I arrive at base."

Their hug was long and silent.  Walter Lucci's rocket flight to the moon had a smooth launch from the William Jefferson Clinton Space Center at 0400 July 7, 2035.

# THREE

It was clear that by the age of three, young Chad was, by nature, precocious and very lovable. Alden had adopted Chad as a single parent in 2043. If it was raining, Chad was happy. If the sun blazed till he had to squint, Chad was happy. If a loved one left on travel, Chad would get teary. And Chad loved to snuggle.

Jessi knelt to meet him eye to eye.

"Chad your Daddy will be waiting for us at 'Randolph's' for tea. Let's go."

It was a short ride by personal escort. 'Randolph's Fine Tea & Pastry House' was where Jessi often brought Chad for Alden to pick him up. The days that Jessi shared with Alden's son were precious to her. Prior to Chad's adoption Alden had tried in every way known to a man to capture the love of Jessi. All his attempts to move the relationship toward romantic love were futile. Alden was resigned to the fact that waves of depression were to blame for her lack of ability to accept the affection that he so longed to shower upon her.

With her Master's degree in European history and sociology completed, Jessi was employed by an historical journalism company that published the online magazine 'Timeless'. The publication, based in Manhattan, had an international audience. Jessi was working towards a job in the editing department, but knew that worldwide competition was keen. Research was her field of expertise. Thus far fifteen of her articles had been published in 'Timeless'.

"Jessi, look at the strudel!"

Chad was making squiggly lines in the frosting of his Danish pastry. Jessi found herself feeling a moment of quiet déjà vu. Once again it left her longing to know why she so often felt a searching for part of herself … a part of herself that she feared had died.

"Chad, here's your dad."

As usual, Alden was grinning and also, as usual, appearing a little awkward.

"And here is a birthday surprise for our Jessi."

Alden placed a small butter cream cake on the table. It was decorated with one candle. With a gentle kiss and a whisper in her ear, Jessi was reminded that today was her 34th birthday. It was December 4th, 2045.

Lauren arrived at Jessi's apartment at 6pm. Not expecting her daughter to be home from work, she pressed her fingerprint onto the door's scanning panel. After stepping over a toy spaceship and a silicone ball with details of the Earth's moon topography, she sat a small boxed cake on the counter.

There was music coming from the bedroom.

"Jessi, it's Mom. I didn't think you'd be here yet."

Lauren walked into the room. Jessi was sitting on the edge of the bed, staring forward, with a blank affect. There was no recognition in her eyes and there was no response to Lauren's presence. Jessi was in a catatonic state.

The medical stabilization team of Emerg-Evac transported Jessi from the landing area atop her apartment building to Grace Hospital. Charles was in his office on the sixth floor of the hospital, talking frantically with Lauren on video phone. Both of Jessica's parents had feared that this was perhaps the outcome of her latest depressive episode. They had recently been counseled by the team of psychiatrists and were advised that it was not safe for Jessi to be living alone.

Lauren and Charles had pleaded with her to move back to Skyscape Towers with them. Jessi's proverbial excuse was the two days a week that Chad spent at her apartment, plus there were numerous, immature expressions of denial that Charles and Lauren could not penetrate. None of that mattered now. Jessi spent the evening of her 34th birthday at Grace Hospital.

Charles Warren and Dr. Wayne Brennan had been close friends since Wayne joined the neurology staff at

Grace Hospital in 2033. Charles had discussed Jessi's case with Wayne on numerous occasions, and felt deep respect for his knowledge and conservative practice as a neurologist. Today's meeting in Wayne's office was tense.

"Charles, when I made rounds with the treatment team today, we discussed the possibility of cold micro-wave cortex stimulation for Jessica. CMCS has been used twice at Grace in the past three months. In the first case of a 64 year old man with grade 4 catatonia, there was a complete reversal of symptoms. Cognitive functioning was superior to his scores preceding the catatonic episode. However, in the case involving a 56 year old woman, the results were not as spectacular. Following treatment, the patient is attending to her personal hygiene and feeds herself. She is still aphasic. Right now she is at our Progressive Center on Long Island."

"Just what is the CMCS procedure, Wayne? Is it approved or still considered research?"

"The procedure has passed all the FMB requirements but official sanction has not been given to end the research status. The delicacy of the vascular mapping is where the procedure has come under the most scrutiny. The entire brain is thoroughly scanned and computer generated mapping is studied. Radioactive isotopes are traced through the vascular area of the cortex. Vascular areas must be avoided during the procedure. A cerebral vascular accident could result if the microwaves should shear any vessels. Basically, the microwaves are introduced through ports that are surgically placed into the cortex of the brain. The waves create new neuro pathways leading from the deeper cortex to the higher cortex. The average person uses only a small percent of their cortex for thought processing, so the unused portion is available for new pathways that we believe are stimulated into activity by the cold microwave. The results of the procedure have been astonishing to the field of neurology. But Charles, there are risks. There are always risks."

⌒

"Mom's gone now. I have to do something different, Justin. I'm going to the Lunar Colony."

"What are you going to do there that we're not doing here?"

Fernando took a shot of whiskey and swirled it across his tongue.

"Zandia Excavating has hired me. I'm gonna do the same thing that I have been doing here. But this time I'm going to find out why I feel so damn incomplete. I think it has more to do with just the loneliness I've felt since Mom died. No matter how many search and rescues I have done, I'm just plain ol' lost to why I feel so empty."

Justin leaned back and took a long drag from a joint of marijuana.

"I see you on a ship, Nando. I see you so clear. On a ship. Maybe it's a space ship, Nando."

On December 4th, 2049, Fernando Welsh left, via shuttle, for the lunar surface.

⌒

"Chad, we'll go sit with Jessi tomorrow."

Alden was seated at his monitor completing work that he knew should have been finished a week earlier. He was working for Insta Data. Many mergers of major software corporations had occurred and dissolved since 2044. Alden glanced at the date on his monitor. It was December 3rd 2050.

"OK, Dad but don't forget 'cause I got her a birthday present."

Nine-year-old Chad abruptly left Alden's home office to retreat to his world of spaceship models and sci-fi computer games.

Alden closed the monitor and gazed into the blackness. The environmental sensor slowly amplified the light in the room until Alden's verbal command stopped the increasing light and sent the automatic dimmer into action. Despite knowing that three shots of cognac were too much for him, Alden poured himself another, and lit a full enhanced joint. Marijuana was now commonly enhanced with herbs such as valerian to add a tranquilizing effect, or other herbs, like gingko, for a mental lift.

By 2050 there were consciousness expanders that had an effect similar to the attributes of the old formula for LSD. But the legal variety was self-limiting. Alden's dad Walter always joked that he could expand his consciousness higher smoking catnip. Alden smiled as he thought about his dad. Walter had retired from active duty with the Lunar Colony division of NASA three years ago. He was now a highly compensated consultant for private space industries.

Alden was caught unawares by the screen's sudden return to light and the appearance of Walter's image.

"Hey, son. Slackin' off on the job, huh?"

The power and gentleness of Walter Lucci's smile could send a person to the moon.

"Hey, Pops. I'm kinda' stoned."

"Well, I'm looking around this apartment here and nobody gives a damn. Don't tell me that you do!"

Alden could not contain his laughter. "Oh crap. Don't tell me that Mom doesn't care anymore if I get stoned and drunk on top of it!"

"Hate to shock you son, but she hasn't given a damn since you turned twenty one. You are just about twenty one years late in getting that clarified."

There was a shared moment of love between the two men that left them both quiet. Walter interrupted the stillness.

"How is Jessi?"

"The same, Pops."

"Well, I was just notified that a commercial group is starting excavation on the Italiano lunar crater. That place where I buried Jessi's schooner model is so far removed from the populated areas that I never thought in my lifetime that the crater would be touched. In fact I marveled at Jessi's ability to know how remote the Italiano crater was. I'll keep an eye on the video feed and let you know if the case gets lifted. I put it down 'til I hit hard bedrock. I would have dug deeper, but in those days it was all I could do to get out of scanning range for a few hours."

"Thanks Pops. Hard to believe that old case with the burned out schooner is still on your mind."

"Well, you know how I have always felt about Jessica. Now ... yell at my grandson to get in here and talk to his ol' Grandpa."

"Here, Jessi. Happy birthday."

Chad set a small, detailed globe of the Earth's moon onto Jessi's bedside table.

"I think she likes it, Dad."

"I'm sure she does, Chad."


Jessi's room at Joseph Murphy Healing Center was bathed in a warm glow from natural lighting that provided replication of sunrays. There were fresh orchids contained in a bloomotic preserver on the table with a card that read, "For Jessi, happy birthday, with all our love, Mom and Dad."

Alden drew a chair up to Jessi's bedside while Chad, at the window, scoped out a nearby building with his port-tel digital scope.

"Chad, turn that off. Electronics used in this building can interfere with patient monitoring."

"Oh Dad, that was in ancient history. These waves are 7 point 8 Dig-A's and they stream on a frequency similar to 8 point 4's. It is so different from the frequency of monitronics. Those are only a 4 point 1 ... or point 2 at the highest."

"Chad, I have just about had enough of your intellectual defenses and I insist that you turn that scope off immediately."

Chad bounded to Jessi's bedside and touched her arm gently.

"When you wake up Jessi, you and me are gonna' go to the lunar colony with Grandpa and I'll show you a view of Earth from this very scope."

Alden felt a strange emptiness as he tried to shake the thoughts that were stealing into his   conscious awareness. He was resisting the thought that this shell of what Jessi had been was no longer what he desired. The void echoed through Alden's mind and heart. It was difficult to recall a time when he had felt affection for her. He had forgotten the color of her eyes. The sound of her voice was lost to him in a frenzy of new female voices that he heard swimming in his mind. The desire for Jessi's body had been replaced by the attraction that he felt for women in each new day of his life.

Chad turned to Alden and firmly stated, "Dad, I know you don't love her anymore, but me and Gramps do. If I was old enough I would take her out of this sterile crypt and take her home and read stories to her and show her the Italiano crater ... "

"That's enough Chad. We're going home now."

The ride in the descending tube was silent. Alden was now aware of his greatest fear. Chad was as tele-pathically developed as Jessi had been and he had immediately felt his father's disquieting revelation.

"Dad, I want to live with Grandpa."

Alden's retort was quick and sharp.

"Chad that will never happen no matter what mind games you try to play. In my earlier days a kid wouldn't start acting out like you are right now, not until he was at least fifteen. My thoughts about Jessi are my own and none of your business. Get that clear son. You will not bring electronics into this medical building again. If you do, I will store all of your apps on the Zettabyte field and bar access to them until you turn twelve."

⌒

"Charles, we should have made a hologram for Jessi this Christmas."

"It's not too late to find one. I'll look online and choose one to be sent electronically to the screen in her room."

Charles kissed Lauren gently and left their apartment. Accepting the prognosis that Jessi would remain comatose for the rest of her life, Lauren had resolved to not abandon her daughter. The procedure of cold microwave cortex stimulation had resulted in a cerebral hemorrhage that left Jessi nonresponsive to all external stimuli. It had taken both Lauren and Charles years to accept the medical facts. It had taken five very long years.

Lauren's satellite phone was signaling her to answer.

"Hello Lauren. This is Kaylyn."

"Kaylyn how wonderful to hear your voice. Where are you? I don't recognize the code displayed?"

"I'm in Venice. It is remarkably beautiful here in December, but it's unbelievably cold!"

"What brought you there?"

"My work with Trav-Com. I am in their marketing and PR division now. We're booking reservations to the Galaxy Resort on the lunar crater Italiano. They broke ground on the excavation earlier this month and plan to open for tourism late next year. Can I book you and Charles a trip?"

Lauren laughed.

"Charles and I spent our wedding anniversary on the moon two years ago. With the exception of the astonishing view into the solar system and the Earth looming there like a giant, weightless balloon, I would rather spend my time on Earth!"

"Lauren, I found a holocard of 'Venice at Dusk'. The audio is lovely. Do you remember the song 'The Air That I Breathe'?"

"Oh yes. That song was a favorite of my mother's. I got tingles just as you said that."

"Well, the holocard has a background of Monet's 'Venice at Dusk'. There is a striking nineteenth century schooner sailing toward the harbor. It is magnificent, Lauren. I want Jessi to have it in her room. May I send it to you and Charles electronically?"

Lauren could not contain her tears. "Please do Kaylyn. Thank you. Please."

So it was, that on Christmas Eve 2050, Walter Lucci sat cushioned at Jessi's bedside in a cozy recliner, feeling rested in the ambiance of replicated natural solar rays. On the large screen was the hologram of Venice at Dusk with a magnificent schooner sailing proudly, masts erect and sails filled tight with wind. Walter dozed off to sleep as the environ-control eased into a simulation of dusk. The room gently darkened, creating a blazing crimson scene on the screen displaying one of Claude Monet's finest expressions. From the audio stream came the melody and words sung in Italian...

"Sometimes, all I need is the air that I breathe ... and to love you ..."

It was time for Jessi to return from her scheduled daily hyperbolic therapy. She was wheeled into the room by the patient care technician.

"Merry Christmas, Mr. Lucci. Isn't that hologram gorgeous? It came on the screen just as I was transporting Jessica to therapy."

Walter was beginning to snore lightly as the tech quickly transferred Jessi to her bed via the digitalized Lif-Trans. After arranging the coverlet and reconnecting the nutrition tube and urinary flow container, she quietly left the room. Simulated starlight gradually appeared on the ceiling above Jessi's bed. Visiting hours ended at Joseph Murphy Healing Center at 10 pm. Walt woke with a start as the soft female voice on the intercom announced the hour as 21:30. With a slow stretch and yawn, Walter glanced at Jessi. She appeared to be asleep. Walter stood to his feet and reached for his coat on the foot of Jessi's bed.

"Armi … where …"

Jessi was whispering. Her eyes were slightly open. Walter leaned his head close to her lips.

"Yes, Jessi. What did you say?"

"Armi … where … where is Feder … Armister … where is Federico."

Charles was frantic.

"What did she say, Walt? Is she awake? My God in heaven!"

"Before you and Lauren go in the room to see her, I need to tell you more …"

Charles interrupted Walt in mid sentence.

"All I need is to see her!"

Lauren was tearful and pacing the hall in front of Jessi's room.

"Charles!  Listen to Walt.  We have waited for five years to see Jessi awake, and you are being harsh and rude."

"I'm sorry, Walter.  I am so grateful that you phoned before Jessi's doctor or the staff did.  I am very sorry.  I was behaving like a mad man!  Please, let's sit here."

Charles motioned to a sitting area off the hallway.  When Lauren and Charles were seated Walter attempted to resume talking.

"Jessi doesn't recognize me.  But she is waking up and spoke to me.  She called me ..."

"She doesn't recognize you!"

Charles was on his feet.

"Charles, you have to let me finish speaking.  She thinks I am someone else.  She called me Armister.  The staff called Dr. Brennan to come in and see Jessi, and Dr. Harvey, on staff here at the center, is with her right now."

"Oh, God.  Oh, God."

Charles began pacing.  Lauren then sat down in a chair, her head bent and hands covering her face.  Walter Lucci's hands were trembling as he placed them on Lauren's shoulders.

"This doesn't mean that she won't recognize you and Charles, Lauren.  You can just imagine how fuzzy her thought processes would be after these years of being in a coma. Her eyes were partly open and she looked straight at me when she spoke."

Charles reversed the direction of his pacing.

"Did she move her head or any of her limbs?"

"No. Her voice was barely a whisper. But she repeated her words until I could hear her clearly."

"Come on, Walter. What did she say?"

Lauren stood.

"Charles, you need more than to see Jessi. You need to shut up and listen to Walter. Walt, please forgive Charles. He is clearly in shock."

"I can only imagine how you and Charles feel. This is a miracle and I am still rather breathless myself. Jessi called me Armi ... then Armister. She asked me where Federico is."

"Thank God. She is going to be fine. Federico is the name of that Italian who had the model made of his schooner. The model was in a bottle that burst and burned. You remember don't you Lauren."

"Of course, Charles."

With an extension of his hand to Charles and a kiss to Lauren's cheek, Walter, exhibiting his usual wisdom and grace, quietly left Charles and Lauren to their privacy. Jessi's parents now left alone in the hall, staring at each other, found themselves totally unprepared for this turn of events.

"We've got several inches of dust and then four feet of sand in this area before we hit bedrock. John Bayer will operate the scoop robot from reference point 57A to 66A. Note that the area is marked with red flags on poles. The soil will be ejected into open pit 22. We need all six of our environ dust robots activated for compression of particles. Ron Porter will assign a crew of three men to each blow force robot for directing dust toward the compressors. All Zandia excavating employees will find detailed information regarding this crater by entering code 8883 Crater Italiano at Zandia Base 89. Thank you all and have a safe shift today. Replacement party chief Sharde will provide the relief crew their shift instructions."

Fernando Welsh left the Zandia communications area. He entered the safety suit section to be assisted by the environ-uniform division of Zandia.

By the year 2050 environmental uniforms had been streamlined to remarkable flexibility and movement. With the advent of new synthetic heat resistant materials, the burden and encumbrance of the older space suit models was obsolete. Oxygen packs were digitalized and each inhalation was computerized for the exact O2 dispersion per minute. The packs were now as small as an average sized satellite phone.

The storage capacity for twelve hours of oxygen consumption at the rate of two liters per minute included the ideal combination of all gasses for sustaining life.

Oxygen from photosynthesis was produced on the moon by cultivating green algae and cyanobacteria in giant bio domes on the lunar surface that was exposed to light.

As Nando entered the decontamination section his uniform was radiated to destroy all contaminates. He stepped into the exit area, appreciative of the new optic aids in his face screen helmet. They brought a whole new view to space walking. The peripheral optic view was a complete wrap around effect. By lowering the eye's vision toward the lower portion of the face shield, readings of the geological conditions being viewed were translated onto a small screen located in the middle of the face shield. A few clicks of a device secured to the front of the uniform returned the optic viewer to regular eye vision.

Nando stepped into the low gravity experience of moon walking with a smile beaming through his face shield. It was his job as party chief to observe the crews as they worked, and to provide a direct communication line with the Zandia main office located within the bio-sphere perched on the edge of Crater Italiano. He approached the parameter and noticed one of the red flags intended to mark the specific area to be excavated had fallen from its position and was lying horizontal in the stillness. Nando reached to lift the pole and proceeded to replace it deeply into the gravelly sand. The repositioning was unsuccessful as the pole slowly leaned and fell into the dust.

"I need a robot dig over here at 66A. Please respond."

Within a few moments a robot slid smoothly toward the direction of his call. Nando entered the commands 'dig', 'scoop' and 'retreat after covering a dig of four square feet'. The robot was silent in its work. With amazing dexterity, the robot excavated an acrylic case containing bits of wood held within a mound of ashes. Nando lifted the retrieved object and selected 'magnification' on his optic face shield. It was clearly the burned hull of a sea sailing ship model from Earth. Splintered glass particles had been mounted onto ashes and treated in such a manner that those ashes congealed into a mound. The fore of the ship was intact. The words 'My Jessica' appeared ... scorched, yet visible. Gripping the case with both hands, a shiver vibrated to the very core of Fernando Welsh's being.

⌒

"Mr. and Mrs. Warren, I'm Dr. Victor Hughes from the neuropsychiatric department here at Murphy Center."

The doctor's cheerful spirit filled his face. He extended his hand to Lauren, then to Charles. The three were seated in a comfortable conference room near Murphy Center's administrative offices, where Lauren and Charles had been encouraged by the staff to wait.

"I am delighted to tell you that Jessica is experiencing a normal brain wave pattern of natural sleep as of this hour. Every one of the staff here at Murphy, including Dr. Wayne Brennan of Grace Hospital, is appreciative of your patience this morning. I know you have been here throughout the night and must be exhausted."

"We are fine Dr. Hughes. But we want so badly to just see Jessi."

Lauren tried to smile through her tears. Charles was finally quiet, and listening. Dr. Brennan had arranged for Charles to receive a prescription for calming medication. For that, Lauren was also grateful.

"I will begin by explaining her physiological condition and then Dr. Brennan will join us on the screen for a conference regarding his up-to-date psychological findings. This meeting will be video recorded in its entirety for the purpose of establishing the medical record."

Lauren and Charles sat transfixed as details of the medical findings regarding Jessi's condition unfolded before them. All body organ systems were functioning. Her cardio-vascular system was profoundly strong, considering the five year period of a comatose status. Neurological reflexes were normal. Muscular strength was inadequate, but expected to increase with therapy. Bone density had been preserved and renal function and gastrointestinal function had been maintained.

Charles took notes regarding the hematological readings. The blood chemistries were all within normal range. He noted that even the serum serotonin level was normal. Jessi had never had a normal serotonin reading. Her body's inability to respond to any of the advanced serotonin re-uptake inhibitors had always been the diagnostic basis for the repeating episodes of severe depression.

When the conference regarding Jessi's condition was completed, Lauren and Charles were permitted to see her from a one way viewing glass. Their daughter Jessica appeared to be sleeping.

⌒

"Look at this, John. Look at the beauty of this."

John Bayer took the acrylic case from Nando's hands. He placed it under a magnifying scope container, one that immediately brought the magnified image up for screen viewing.

"Well, Nando, it looks like a half burned up model of an old Earth sea ship and it looks like it was named 'My Jessica'. Where did you get this?"

"I found it out in the crater. It was meant to be that I found it. I feel an immediate connection with this ship."

"Hey Nando. Wait just a minute. Where are you comin' from man?"

John stared at the magnification and turned again to Nando.

"Are you oxygen deprived?"

"No, John. I know what it's like to zone out while working in the lunar environment with sole dependency on our environ-control equipment. This isn't like that. This model ship, half burned as it is, was encased in a glass bottle at one time and I know this ship was mine. It's my schooner and I named it after a woman. And I also know that I loved her like no other woman, ever."

"OK, Nando. That makes your sweet ass way over one hundred and fifty years old plus or minus several decades. You don't look much over forty to me dude. Tell me more. This is intriguing."

"If you will stop the sarcasm John, I just might tell you more."

"OK, go for it man. I'm listening. But I must tell you that this crap sounds a bit crazy. Let's go to the Galaxy Bar and have a few shots. I'll give both my ears for you to bend."

⌒

After arriving back at their apartment at Skyscape Towers on Christmas Day, Lauren and Charles found sleep impossible. Charles had adjusted the control to replicate midnight. He reached for a glass bottle of cognac on the wet bar and poured several ounces into a snifter. Lauren was curled on her side under the bed covers, but her eyes were wide open. It was 2 pm.

"Wayne's idea that we shouldn't see Jessi until she is more prepared to see us is preposterous! Her amnesia would be helped by our presence right now!"

Charles reached again for the cognac bottle. Lauren remained quiet.

"And the idea that if you and I walked into her room today, Jessi could have a psychotic break because she wouldn't know us? Well! That's just too much to take! Lauren, you tell me. Am I the one losing my mind now?"

"No darling. You are just not considering all the implications of her fragile mental state."

"Well, I most certainly have considered such matters. Jessica is our daughter. We have rights as her legal guardians to see her anytime we want to! Don't you see it that way?"

Lauren stared at Charles.

"Not entirely Charles. This is not 2011. It is almost 2051. Today, consideration of the patient's wellbeing is established by the attending physicians. That outweighs the wishes of the guardian unless overturned by a Federal Judge. You of all people should know that. Especially you, Charles! You have been a CEO of a major hospital all of these years. I haven't practiced law for ten years. Maybe it's me who's losing my mind? We must be patient Charles. Jessi's treatment will be decided by her treatment team. We are cleared to observe some of her therapies through the one way glass. Just think we'll be able to hear her speak. And see her smile. Oh ... I am so grateful!"

Charles began to snore loudly. He had passed out.

"It makes no sense to me! Armister was here and he would never leave me with people I don't know."

Jessi began to cry. Dr. Brennan elevated the head of her bed and repeated himself softly.

"Jessica, this is the year 2050. It is Christmas Day. You are on Long Island in New York. My name is Dr. Wayne Brennan. You are waking up after a long period of unconsciousness."

"No! That is not true. It is nineteen hundred something. I am dreaming. Where is Federico?"

Jessi moved her legs towards the side of the bed, tugging at the gastric feeding tube and urinary catheter.

"Ouch! That hurts. What is this rope?"

Panic stricken, she attempted to stand. Dr. Brennan caught her in his arms just as she slumped to the floor. The door opened and two techs and an RN entered the room.

"We will have to sedate her again. Give her Comforian 10 milligrams, IM. When she is sedated, remove the catheter and clamp the gastric tube. I didn't want to put her in a safe room. But I don't think we have a choice."

The Berlshire Hotel was among the finest in New York City. Alden and Chad ascended the tube to the 75th story, to the 'members-only' dining room.

"Dad this is the fastest tube ride I've ever had. Are Grandma and Grandpa here yet?"

"I don't know Chad. We will be seated either way."

Alden's mood was blunted. He was hoping that his Pops would not make every toast that day to Jessi's awakening, but he had pretty much resigned to the fact. The tube opened onto a three story atrium filled with exotic trees representing five continents of Earth. Lush gardens, with the pungent aroma of orchids and English tea roses, lined the marble tiled path. Alden placed his palm onto the scanner and the wrought iron garden gate opened, complete with a squeaky sound effect that Chad found fascinating.

"Wow. That *is* radasonic!"

After a walk through the atrium garden to the dining room, Chad and Alden were escorted by the service staff to the Lucci table. Walter and Marge stood for hugs. Both were beaming with holiday cheer.

"This is truly beautiful, Mom. You and Pops have clearly impressed your grandson."

Each linen covered table was adorned with a bouquet of scarlet Don Juan roses, trimmed with silk green ribbon. Soft candle light flickered through the leaded crystal centerpiece. Walter told the waiter that he wished to pour the wine. Walter stood and poured a sip for approval by Alden, then filled the glasses. There was another bottle chilling in silver at table side. He lifted the loosened cork from a bottle of California grape juice and poured his grandson a taste. After a smile of approval from Chad, Walter filled the glass.

"Hey! Look! I have my very own bottle!"

Walter raised his glass of wine.

"Oh, here it comes", thought Alden. But Alden was wrong. The Christmas toast was not about Jessi's awakening.

Walt toasted. "Here's to love."


Dr. Victor Hughes was the physician on staff at Joseph Murphy Healing Center on Christmas night. His satellite phone signaled him.

"Vic, this is Wayne Brennan. Have the staff moved Jessica Warren to a safe room yet?"

"Not yet, Wayne, but we are about ready to. She's asleep."

"Damn, I hate to move her. Do you see any other option for her safety Vic?"

Dr. Hughes was feeling the stress of the day and paused.

"Well, we could try a nurse in the room with her, one-to-one. We have back up staff available at a moment's notice. Right now she is being monitored through the one way glass. But like you, I'm concerned about her falling. I don't think she has the physical strength to get violent and hurt herself with objects in there but do you want to try a nurse 'round the clock?"

Wayne Brennan let out a long sigh.

"Put your best nurses in there twenty four hours a day, Vic. Thank you man! Merry Christmas and I'll be over in the morning. By the way, in case you haven't had a chance to pull up all of Jessica's medical record Vic, I am the surgeon who did the CMCS on her five years ago. I just got the best Christmas present of my life last night."

Olivia Bradshaw RN was from the old school of the 2020's. Robust and rotund, she had seen it all. A psych nurse from Grace Hospital before she joined the staff at Joseph Murphy Healing Center in 2043, Olivia was one of 'the best' that Dr. Brennan said he wanted to be one-to-one with Jessi.

Dr. Hughes felt confident in choosing her for the assignment.

"Tough, but smart, with good old fashioned wisdom," Vic thought to himself. "I have picked number one."

Dr. Victor Hughes watched through the one-way glass as Olivia approached Jessi's bedside.

Olivia RN spent Christmas night by Jessi's side. The hologram on the screen had remained closed since shortly after Jessi had woken on Christmas Eve. At dawn, Olivia opened the screen and set the hologram for continuous play. A blazing crimson scene of Monet's 'Venice at Dusk' filled the five foot screen. The proud schooner sailed in three dimensions through the room.

The Italian vocal was set on soft play and flowed gently from the sound system.

"…a volte …ho bisogno di tutti e presente aria che respiriamo …..e ad amare te."

(Sometimes ... all I need is the air that I breathe ... and to love you.)

"Look, I told you. There is the Liberty."

Jessi was awake. She slowly reached her arms a few inches toward the 3-D image at the foot of the bed.

"Hello Jessica. I'm Olivia."

"Auntie Olivia? You look different. Where is Armi? He was here. I think he went to find Federico. I feel so weak ..."

"You are going to be just fine Jessica. You will get stronger every day. We are going to help you."

"You and Armi?"

"I don't know who Armi is."

"Your husband Auntie. Armi is your husband. This can't be happening. I must be dead."

"You are very much alive, Jessica. I can assure you that you are alive and doing very well. Thoughts will be confusing for a while, but you will begin to remember all that is important for you to remember. Here is a drink of fruit juice. Try it."

Jessi's therapy began at that moment. There was no challenge of Jessi's words or perceptions. Olivia began to spin an emotional environment that would provide a safety net for the young woman as she explored her new physical world. That was the beginning of the much needed trust building.

Dr. Wayne Brennan listened through the speaker system and watched the scene through the one-way glass. After a sip of coffee he turned from the viewing window and walked away. The day treatment team was preparing to relieve the night staff.

"What did Dr. Brennan say as he was leaving?"

"Not sure, but I think he said 'Thank God'."

Charles managed to ease his hangover with an herbal tea combination that Lauren had blended for him.

"Darling, can you forgive me for my behavior yesterday?"

"Charles, you were in shock to learn of Jessi waking up. I am still so very shaky. We just handle some things differently. Enough said about yesterday."

"I'm going on into the office and try to behave in the manner that my loving family well deserves."

Charles' phone signaled him.

"Wayne. Thanks for calling. Any news regarding Jessi today?"

"I met with the treatment team at Murphy Center this morning. Jessica was sedated last evening. She is doing well, but she got very agitated when she discovered the feeding tube. We have begun to help her address her confused thought processes by having a psychiatric nurse stay in the room with her around the clock. The nurses will spend twelve hour shifts, one to one with her. She is eating a soft diet and tolerating it well. Charles, I am so delighted with her physical condition. Mentally she is living in what appears to be a fantasy of the early 1900's. Her amnesia is severe. Dr. Hughes and I are hoping that we can safely bring you and Lauren into Jessica's world very soon. But I need to prepare you for the likely possibility that she will not recognize you. Her delusional state of mind might be difficult to accept."

"Thank you Wayne, but Lauren and I are ready to see our Jessi exactly as she appears right now."

"I am glad to hear that Charles. Please plan on a Murphy Center staff coordinated meeting regarding Jessica. The staff will phone you within a few days and meanwhile, Dr. Victor Hughes is going to arrange a live stream video conference between you and Lauren and one of the nurses at Murphy Center. I believe her name is Olivia."

Olivia Bradshaw pulled up a chair to Jessi's bedside and reached for her hand.

"Do you know how I got here, Olivia? I don't remember. But I am beginning to remember some things. I will be so happy when Federico and I are together again."

Olivia hesitated a moment before answering Jessi's question.

"Jessica I do know that you are getting much stronger. You're doing very well. I'll have a white board placed on the wall here in your room. We will write the day's activities on the board each morning, as well as the correct date and the times you will be working with different hospital staff on your healing therapies."

"What does therapies mean?"

"Therapy means any activity you do that helps you gain physical strength, helps you have peace of mind."

# FOUR

"Jessi, look at the geese!"

Chad held Jessi's hand to support her as they made their way slowly down to the water's edge. As a result of lengthy physical therapy and her determination to regain muscle strength, Jessi was making steady progress. A flock of Canadian geese rose into flight, spraying the pair with drops of lake water. Chad began tugging at Jessi's hand.

"Oh Chad, I am so out of breath. Please slow down. I am really still very unsteady on my feet. One day I might be able to run again. Then we will race, and I might even win. But first, I must learn to walk".

April in Central Park was cool and breezy. Tiny green buds pushed through the smallest twigs of the trees. Chad found a patch of snow under a cherry tree. After moving a mound of the crusty stuff to a clearing, his fingers made lunar-like craters on its surface. In moments he was preparing to launch his model rocket. Jessi walked slowly back to the park bench and sat next to Walt.

"Walter, is Chad really going to fly that?"

Walter smiled that huge warm smile that could have melted every last spot of snow in New York City had that been his intent.

"Yes Jessi, but the rocket is programmed to go up just a few hundred feet and then come slowly back down to the launch pad. The rocket has a chute that will open at a certain altitude. The chute will open sooner if the rocket hits any obstruction. For example, if the rocket should hit the hand of the person launching it, or their face ... or a tree branch ... there is an immediate de-escalation of force. The rocket is almost weightless. The toy is based on the old principles of programmed rocket flight, but without any fuel propellant of course."

Walter suddenly realized that Jessi probably had no understanding of what he had just said. Jessi was staring as Chad's rocket lifted off.

"It went so fast I hardly saw it happen."

Almost before Jessi completed her sentence, the rocket model could be seen high above the trees, slowly descending under a bright yellow chute. Chad was busy preparing the pad for another launch.

"I remember my first trip into space. It was before you were born, Jessi. I looked back at our planet Earth and never quite felt the same about life again."

"What did you see, Walter?"

"I saw ... that all people ... are part of a much bigger plan in the universe than we are aware of in our very limited lives on Earth."

Chad re-launched the rocket and Jessi and Walter remembered to applaud that time.

As the three rode back to Skyscape Towers via private escort, Jessi reached for Walter's hand.

"Walter, something tells me that it is alright to talk to you about Federico. I have been asked to learn all these new things and not keep asking about Federico. But is it alright if sometimes ... I just talk to you about him?"

Walter slowly nodded.

Chad broke the silence.

"Jessi, you can talk to me about Federico anytime you want to."

"Well, Chad, I recall the time when Federico came to my Auntie Olivia's apartment in New York. He had come to call for the third ... or maybe it was the fourth, time. We sat in the parlor and he gave me a package wrapped in fine indigo silk. Inside were two Venetian glass bottles, a glass that came from fire. They glowed with a brilliant purple hue."

"Oh, Jessi, that is so rad cool. Do you still have the bottles?"

Jessi turned to Walter who was staring out the window of the escort. After a long pause, she turned back to Chad.

"That is a very good question. I don't really remember what happened to them. But wherever they are, I know they aren't broken, but maybe cracked a little."

"Lauren, who did you tell me Katherine Lynne was?"

Lauren had adjusted to the fact that Jessi could not identify her as her mother, nor call her Mom.

"Her name is Kaylyn, Jessi. She is a very good friend of the family. You knew her well. You grew up together. I worked with her mother when you girls were babies."

"You said she has been in Venice? Maybe she has seen Federico. We lived in Venice for a time. Did I tell you that Federico was born in Rome?"

"Yes Jessi, you did tell me that. Kaylyn will be here any minute. Could you help me slice the butter cake?"

At that moment the chimes sounded and Kaylyn danced into the foyer.

"Wow! My print still works on the scanner."

Lauren ran to the foyer and embraced Kaylyn.

"Kaylyn, you look absolutely beautiful! Come in here and see Jessi. We have been making a little cake to have with tea."

Jessi was arranging cake slices on the serving platter as Kaylyn entered the dining room.

"Hi Jessi, I'm Kaylyn. It's so good to see you again."

There were tears in Kaylyn's eyes.

"It is very nice to meet you. Are you feeling sad?"

"No, Jessi, I'm happy to see you. These tears, they are tears of happiness."

Lauren served tea. The three women sat in awkward silence for a few minutes. Lauren began nervous chatter about Venice but soon regretted bringing up the subject. Jessi spoke right up.

"Did you see Federico de Silva in Venice?"

Kaylyn sipped her tea and looked at Lauren who was picking at her slice of cake with a fork.

"No. I didn't meet any one in Venice by that name."

"Did you see Claude Monet? He's a very fine painter. He is painting seascapes of Venice. Federico introduced us. He painted me in a field holding a perc ... oh, I forgot the word. You know like an umberb ... oh, I forgot that word too."

Jessi was flushed and sweating. Lauren stood quickly.

"It is all alright Jessi. My dear sweet Jessi."

Kaylyn rose to her feet and gently squeezed Jessi by the shoulders as she whispered into her ear.

"It is all very alright. You will always be my best friend."

⌒

Twice a week Jessi attended therapy at Joseph Murphy Healing Center, as an outpatient. Lauren always accompanied her and attended family group therapy while Jessi was in private therapy or at one of her group sessions. Today there was a change in routine. Walter Lucci was accompanying Jessi to the center. The private escort service was stalled in traffic.

"Walter, how is Chad?"

"He is very good Jessi. The three of us must have dinner soon."

Walter seemed to be rested and well.

"Will Alden be joining us? I didn't find it easy to converse with him when you introduced me to him, but he is Chad's father. And he is your son. I want to try again to be more socially proper. I am learning many new things. Now I see that I wasn't always proper since I got to New York."

Walter smiled that extraordinary smile.

"Jessi you are always proper. I haven't heard that word for some time."

"What word, Walter?"

"Proper."

The two enjoyed a shared laugh as the private escort began moving across Long Island Bridge.

"Walter, thank you for coming with me today. I just know that you will like Mary. She says that art therapy is for everyone and might ask if you would like to paint a picture too."

The occupational therapy room was spacious. Sunlight shining through the panes of four large French windows sent filtered light across the floor, creating a warm pattern. On a center table Mary had spread out two smooth, wet sheets of paper and placed glasses of water, each tinted with a different pigment. Artist's brushes rested beside containers of clear water, sponges and pieces of cloth.

"Mr. Lucci, it is so helpful when family and friends participate with our clients here at Murphy Center whenever possible. It is a pleasure to meet you."

Jessi had already seated herself comfortably in a cushioned chair at the table. Walter chose the chair alongside her. He squinted to read the titles of some well worn classic books that filled a tall shelf on the back wall. Mary began to speak.

"We don't have any rules in art therapy, except to ask that silence be maintained until the painting has been completed. Please begin this session by closing your eyes for a moment. Take a few deep breaths, and be filled with the atmosphere of peace in this room."

Jessi's shoulders began to relax. The aroma of blooming flowers scented the air. A vase with fresh cut English roses had been placed on a tea cart near the window. Several soft pink petals had fallen to rest on the cart's wooden surface, among the China teacups.

After a few moments, Mary resumed.

"The paper before you has been prepared by moistening with water, so that it has become receptive, like a farmer ploughs a field before he plants the seeds. 'Wet-on-wet' watercolor painting ensures that the colors remain alive and fluid. Edges lose their sharp definition.

Colors flow with rhythm and without effort or struggle, and forms appear ever so subtly. In other words, we allow the color to experience a sense of liberation. Please begin when you are ready and I will rejoin you at the end of the session."

Mary quietly left the room, closing the door softly behind her.

Walter stared at Jessi's paper as a tiny drop of vivid blue dripped from her brush. The diluted color ran in all directions and soon the white paper began to glow beneath a transparent blue veil. Then Jessi introduced drops of yellow, followed by touches of red, each new addition sending patterns swirling across the blue surface as she gently lifted and tilted the edges of the paper. Drops of clear water splashed, like teardrops, into the colors. She was fascinated as the ripples dispersed into new blends, creating the lightest shades of purple and green. The scene unfolded into a fiery sunrise on a horizon of frothy sea water. Jessi added another drop of blue, then another, and more, until they gathered and formed into indigo storm clouds that swept light into darkness. She rested her brush.

"Walter, my father did not want me to be with Federico. He arranged for me to marry an Englishman."

Drawing a long breath and glancing at Walter, Jessica turned back to the seascape on the table in front of her. Her eyes were closed and her voice was barely a whisper.

"I was taken back to Baltimore because Papa had made plans for my future. Federico is a good and honest man. He's the owner of a large European shipping business. But Papa had him investigated and I was sent away.

"I remember being on the ship, going to London, with my Aunt Olivia as my chaperone. We were having luncheon in our cabin when we heard the whistle of cannon fire. Then the purser, Mr. Timmons, ran along the deck, shouting 'Pirates!' I was shaking with fear. Through the porthole we could see three ships. They were flying no jacks, but we could read their names ... 'Freedom', 'Liberty' and 'Valiant''.

"Federico must have learned of my father's plans and ordered three ships to set sail. Our steamship was facing serious damage from the threat of nine cannons, so the captain agreed to Federico's demands.

"Our trunks were packed and I was taken on board the 'Liberty'. Auntie Olivia returned to New York, with Armister, on the 'Valiant'. I think the 'Freedom' turned for Brazil. The 'Liberty' sailed to the Mediterranean. Federico studied the stars. He is very skilled in mathematics and astronomy. The location of a ship at sea can be determined by measuring the moon against the background of stars. Federico spoke of the dangers of poor visibility, of mists and heavy storms, but the moon and stars guided us safely to Venice. That is pretty much how my life with Federico began."

Walter sat motionless. The paper before him remained white and was now dry.

"Perhaps, Walter, you already know these things."

Jessi turned the blank pages of a book that Mary had given her. Trying to recall what Mary had called the book, she noticed that every page was blank. She read the words 'My Journal' scrolled in script across the first cover. The sun had set. It was warmer than Jessi remembered July to be.

*Dear Diary,*

*I am very old. By the date of today, I am one hundred and eighty seven years old. This is quite astonishing to me. Olivia told me I am not dead. But as time goes by, I am afraid that I might be.*

*Lauren says I was born in 2011. I know very well that I was born in Baltimore, Maryland, on December 4th, 1863. Mathematics has never been my skill. However, I am sure that if I am not dead, I am very old.*

*Federico will find me, but maybe it will be hard to find me in these strange clothes. Today I think my hair is getting back right again. It has grown some and touches my breasts like it did before*

*I became ill. Federico will like that my body is strong again. I do not think he will like these clothes.*

*I was so happy when Federico and I were together.*

*~ Jessica*

The host of 'Ristorante DeSarta' led Alden and Jessi to their table. By 2051 most of the buildings in New York were green environ-solartronics. The skyline from their window seat beckoned Jessi to look toward the harbor and from there, out onto the open sea until it melted into the sky.

"You look absolutely lovely tonight, Jessi."

"Thank you, Alden. This is such a beautiful view. The harbor hasn't changed as much as the buildings, but the steamers are huge!"

"Most of those that you can see from here are solar powered."

With Walter's encouragement, Alden had attended several neuropsychology classes at NYU's continuing education campus in Manhattan during the year. He was becoming more comfortable with Jessi's amnesia and her delusional state of mind.

Alden's thoughts drifted. He was thinking about the low scores that Jessi had scored on the intelligence quotient test that he had given her on his computer one evening. Charles had brought Jessi for a visit to see Alden and Chad for the evening at their apartment and Jessi had been fascinated with the solartronics and the immense array of computer equipment that Alden used for his work. That night in early August, Alden sat at the desk monitor and gave Jessi a tour of the solartronic world that spanned the Earth, the lunar colonies and beyond.

Jessi was amazed to see parts of her most secret dreams manifest on a screen. Technology in the year 2051 could legitimately be called a fourth dimensional view of life. Jessi had seemed very comfortable. However, in spite of her courageous efforts to score well during Alden's IQ experiment with her, the results were dismal.

Alden's thoughts were interrupted.

"Alden, have you been to the lunar colonies?"

"Pops took me with him on three of his short runs in the 30's and early 40's. But now they have resorts and huge solar green houses that are biospheres of pure air with a perfect concentration of $O_2$ and $CO_2$. They grow many varieties of plants hydroponically, just as we do here on Earth."

Alden suddenly felt an emotional lift to have Jessi's attention in a way that he had never experienced in her presence before. He became aware of the fact that Jessi no longer used the developed portion of her brain that she had formerly accessed to read his thoughts telepathically. To Alden this was a delightful discovery. When there was no observable change in Jessi's attitude or body posture, Alden tried another experiment. He thought to himself slowly: "Jessi will make a good wife now, because I will teach her how to be a good wife."

Jessi reached for a sip of DeSarta's fine house zinfandel and smiled at Alden.

"Yes Jessi! Here's to the moon! It's time for Chad to take his first ride into real space. The three of us must go soon!"

Alden lifted his wine in toast then poured another, from the glass bottle.

⁓

Charles Warren had built a blazing fire in the marble fireplace in his study. That October was chilly in New York. For many years wood burning had been permitted only if the timber was treated with a solvent that neutralized the smoke. He was feeling a moment of nostalgia as Jessi came closer and gazed into the fire.

"Dad, I love you."

Charles instantly blushed. "What did you say darling?"

"Oh. I don't know. That is strange. Suddenly I thought, um… I felt I had been standing here with you a long time ago. That is a very strange feeling, Charles. I must be tired. And I am getting very old, you know."

"Jessi, you aren't quite forty yet."

After Charles kissed her face gently, Jessi strained as she reached to lift a bronze bust of William Jefferson Clinton from the mantel.

"Here Charles, we should place this on your desk when the fire is burning so high. It might burst."

Shadows of orange and blue flames danced throughout the room and reflected from the arched window that overlooked the city. Charles stepped to his desk.

"Jessi, this is a 2042 issue of 'Timeless' in print form. I have marked one of the articles that you wrote."

"Thank you Charles. Lauren put some copies of the publication in my room. Lauren said I had an apartment of my own here in New York City."

"Yes, you did Jessi. You designed the interior just beautifully. The apartment had a view of the Twin Towers Memorial Park. You are a fine historical journalist. Please read this and you will see just how gifted you are."

Tears spilled from Charles' eyes. There was no response from Jessi.

# GLASS BOTTLES

October 23rd, 2051

Dear Diary,

Tonight I think I know what happened. Some of it is very frightening. Some of it is all right.

I am not dead, but I did die. Federico had sailed to bring an expert physician. Armister and Olivia were with me. We were in our home in Venice, and I was very ill. My hair was white and my body was very thin.

I tried to wait for Federico. I tried so hard, but I failed.

A great relief came over me when I lifted out of my dense body. There was no more pain. I could see Federico crying. But he could not hear me when I told him that I was very fine.

Tonight, I saw pain in Charles' eyes. Then I knew that I am no longer dead. There is no pain in death.

~ Jessica

# GLASS BOTTLES

With the advent of 2020 there had been scientific acceptance of the fact that the explanation of gravity force, as Newton had given the world, was incomplete and not entirely correct. Earlier quantum physics theories had become the normal bases of the ever growing space travel of the 21st Century. All space buff historians had recollection of the great progress that came about through the expansion of environmental studies and the advancement of green technology. Fuel propelled rocket launches had become obsolete by 2024. By '34, all space travel was initiated by shuttles which orbited the Earth at a high velocity until they were literally slung beyond the Earth's atmosphere. How simple the sling shot effect was. Science was still cringing in '45 at the thought that history bore such a primitive record of man's early flight into space. Holes, torn in the ozone layer of the Earth's atmosphere by rocket launches from earlier space travel and placement of thousands of communication satellites, were healed naturally. Ozone replacement, plus radical reduction of green house gas emissions, combined with the world wide use of bio-degradable fuels, was effective. By 2048 billions of Earth inhabitants could look forward to the very probable outcome of the complete end to toxic environmental conditions.

Walter glanced up as a face appeared on the screen.

"Yes, this is Walter Lucci".

"Mr. Lucci, my name is Fernando Welsh. I work for Zandia Lunar Excavating. I have here an old rigger ship model of 'My Jessica'."

Walter was quiet for a moment.

"Well young man, you have un-mooned quite a treasure. I should check you out with Data-International before I speak with you, but something tells me that I don't need to do that. Am I correct about that?"

Without hesitation Nando placed a view of the ship model remains onto the screen. Walter drew a deep breath.

"Name your price young man."

Fernando seemed indignant. His response was firm.

"Mr. Lucci, there is no amount of money that could buy this glass bottle artifact. I know that I have a connection with this ship. If you know, please tell me. Who is this woman named Jessica? I only want to know if she is still alive."

Walter felt as though he was responding from a far away space within himself.

"Yes. Jessica is real. However, for me to tell you the story of the ship within that case, I would need to know you. I would need to know you in a way that few men know each other. The very fact that I am listening to you is beyond my comprehension. If you have a connection with Jessica, I will be assured of that someday. Until such a time that I am convinced, I do not want you to phone me again. I'll be checking on you, Mr. Welsh."

Walter closed the screen, secretly wishing that he could sign off as 'Armister'.

The runway at 'IntraGalact' was the length of one hundred Earth international airports. It sprawled across the Sierra desert in Saudi Arabia. With that length of runway, it was possible to attain a velocity much higher than the speed of sound before liftoff occurred. Saudi Arabia was once known for its oil rich sands. In 2016, with the major emphasis placed worldwide on alternate fuels, the Saudi oil empire was quiet. It was now a teaming reservoir of land for aeronautics and commercial development. Saudi Arabia was a new Mecca of prosperity.

Jessi, Alden, and Chad boarded for takeoff.

"Hey Jessi, just think. We are going' to the moon. I told you we would go to the moon some day ... and here we are."

Chad was squeezing Jessi's hand as they boarded their flight to Lunar Colony Crater Italiano on IntraGalact Orion flight KJ444.

"I know I am only ten now Jessi, but you are my best friend anyway. Happy Birthday."

Alden smiled. It was December 4th 2051. There were few places left on planet Earth where tourists could travel and not be a captive audience of capitalism. A tourist lunar excursion was no exception. Travel to the moon was a prohibited expense for the average middle class citizen. The word class had been deemed politically incorrect by the year 2018. However, that fact did not change the reality. For a lunar tourist, the expectations were well known before their flight left terra firma.

Jessi and Chad were seated together. Before takeoff, Chad read the 'Orion VII' information folder aloud.

1. "No luggage or carryon baggage is permitted.

2. Additional clothing may be purchased from our fine boutiques and shops.

3. Lunar purchases can be shipped to your Earth address for a fee based on the current average exchange rate.

4. Please provide each service person with gratuity commiserate with the services received.

5. A note to our frequent flyers: May we suggest that you lease a storage area for your purchases.

6. The IntraGalact insurance plan is limited to intra-biosphere activities only. For those of our guests

that wish to participate in extro-biosphere activities, please consult with our concierge.

7. To review our full disclosure clause, please see
our disclaimer strip located within each ticket.

Thank you and enjoy your flight and lunar space experience. Sincerely, IntraGalact: Orion VII Space Inc."
Chad lifted his gaze from reading.

"Jessi, Gramps taught me a whole lot about space
launches. We are on a track with a magnetized coil that
makes this ship levitate about a foot above the guide way.
The electric current supplied to the coils is constantly al-
ternating. This means that soon there will be a change in
polarity that will pull us forward real fast. The magnetic
field behind us will add more forward thrust. Jessi, do you
think our faces will peel back when we hit seven G's?"

"Oh Chad, I certainly hope not!"

"This is your Pod Host speaking. Our pilots will soon
de-escalate speed and the passenger    pod will disengage
from the shuttle Orion Seven. As this process occurs you
might experience a slight floating sensation prior to the lunar gate landing. Our pod will be guided into the landing
gate by Luna IntraGalact Port command station. As you
stand upon landing please be prepared to feel a reduction
of your usual body weight. The sensory adjustment to this
feeling of being lighter may or may not occur during your

stay on the lunar surface. It is not an uncomfortable sensation. Thank you for flying Orion Seven. Orion Seven ...
flight IntraGalact KJ444, will commence its return trip to
Earth at 23:00 hours December, 10th, 2051."

Their accommodations at Galaxy Resort on crater
Italiano were mind bending. Each unit was furnished
with four sleeping tubes and individual environ-controls
to choose a temperature range and correct lighting to
please any guest. The soft-to-firm lining of the sleeping tubes could be adjusted by remote control from the
unit's efficiency panel. The main section of the unit was
padded with walls of quilted micro-suede fabric. Sitting
furniture and tables were fixed to the flooring. A large
screen filled one wall of the unit. At that moment it was
displaying the latest NASA photos of Neptune's aqua-
marine, icy surface. Chad bounded over to the observer
section on the other side of their suite.

"Oh look! It's Earth rising!"

Chad was transfixed. The planet Earth was lifting above
the lunar horizon. Bathed in solar light, the planet Earth
loomed in all of its majesty. Swirling hues of blues, greens,
umber and gray slowly rose above the lunar landscape.

"Look, Jessi. You can really see how little the Earth
looks from here."

Jessi was speechless while Alden looked on with
approval. He was far more interested in the view of
his soon-to-be complete family than he was of looking

back to Earth. The guest bar contained a Plexiglas bottle of 'Apollo Spirits'. Alden filled two acrylic stemmed glasses to the brim and tossed Chad an acrylic can of 'Space Gulp', complete with caffeine. Chad was already quite buzzed.

On the fifth day of her adventure to the moon with Alden and Chad, Jessi, familiar with long periods of solitude, found herself alone once again. Alden had arranged to take Chad on what was called an 'exit tour'. They left the biosphere of the Galaxy Resort from a port on the northern side of the dome. Jessi had walked to the pre-exit area with them and hugged them both. There was a strained expression on her face.

"Oh Jessi, Dad took out special insurance for our moon walk. And besides, we are going to be just fine. I'm gonna bounce really high when I get out there. And I'll be waving at you if you wanna watch us on the screen!"

As the heavy doors slid closed, Jessi could barely imagine the idea that there was no air, no wind, not even a breeze where her dear Chad was going. She shuddered at the idea of watching the screen and quickly left the viewing area. Alden had given her a card.

"Jess, you buy whatever you want, in any shop that you want. Money is of no concern. I don't want you to even glance at the price of anything that you buy."

Jessi was still having difficulty understanding the value of the day's currency as it applied to buying things. Alden could have saved his breath regarding instruction to her about money.

Jessi lifted her package up onto the bar.

"Well. Hello. Don't tell me that you are travelling to the moon alone? English?"

Jessi turned as a handsome gentleman eased onto the seat beside her.

"No. I am from Venice, Italy. Currently living in New York."

"How delightful ... is your accent. I don't think I have heard a voice quite like yours. No, I don't think I ever have."

Jessi shyly turned from the stranger's scrutiny.

"May I buy you a drink?"

"Oh, that's quite alright, I can purchase my own."

"Oh, of course you can, but here on the moon it's OK for a man to buy a lady a drink."

"Well ... then do ... whatever is proper, I mean."

Jessi was feeling flushed, remembering that Walter said it had been a long time since he had heard the word 'proper'. What could this man have in mind? She gazed into the glass bottles behind the bar.

"Here, let me lift my glass to ... Venice. *Yes*. To Venice!"

Jessi seemed afraid to move. She was wishing that Walter was with her.

The bartender had placed two glasses of 'Luna Vino 2048' on the bar.

"My name is John Bayer. I am here on the moon with Zandia Excavating."

"Hello. My name is Jessica Goodwin."

Immediately Jessi flushed again and began to stammer.

"Well ... my name is ... now ... it's Warren. Jessica Englund ... Warren. I can't imagine why I said Goodwin. That was a long time ago. Please excuse me. I feel as if I need a little air."

John signaled to the bartender. A nasal cannula and tube, attached to a fixture in the wall behind the bar, was handed to John.

"The O2 is set at 2 liters per minute."

"Here Jessica, you put the tube over your ears. Like this. It goes a little way into your nose, and then adjusts under your chin. Breathe through your nose for a few minutes and you will feel better."

John lightly touched the tips of Jessi's ears and leaned close to adjust the nasal cannula. Jessi could feel his warm breath against her face. John Bayer's timing was flawless. He waited five minutes before resuming the conversation.

"Isn't it amazing how many billions of people have looked up at the moon and wished to find perfect love? When I am working out on the crater I often look at Earth and wish for love."

Jessi was quietly breathing through the O2 cannula and beginning to sip her wine. John had moved closer to her.

"Tell me Jessica what dreams of love brought you to the moon? Or are you here for business?"

The silver blue in Jessi's eyes was glistening.

"Once I knew love. His name is… it was… Federico de Silva. We lived in Venice."

Jessi opened her package on the bar.

"This is a view of Italy from a moon scope. It's framed quite lovely, is it not? Venice is about here."

John touched her hand as she extended her slender finger to the image. His video phone signaled him. After excusing himself, John Bayer walked to the observation area of the lounge.

"Nando, your timing sucks. This is a huge major suck! I have just met a woman that would knock even your socks off man! She is beautiful. Now this better be really good. What are you phoning about?"

"John, I found Walter Lucci! He did bury the old rigger ship model on Italiano crater. I'm sure that Jessica is real and alive, John. Lucci is going to have me checked out and when he finds out that I am clean, I know he'll help me. There's something very familiar about this man Walter Lucci."

"Calm down Nando. You are losing it again, man. I don't mind listening to your stories about your past lives but right now, I am having a glass of wine with a very pretty lady. Later."

John closed the screen of his phone and returned to the bar, only to find that Jessica had left.

"Jessi, look back at the moon!"

Chad was straining for one last look at the lunar surface as IntraGalact flight KJ444 gathered speed and shot toward Earth.

*December 11, 2051*

*Dear Diary,*

*I love Chad so very much. I feel that he is my own child.*

*Tonight I am trying to remember if Federico and I had children. I think we did not. I do not remember why we did not have children. We loved each other more than anything.*

*Alden says we could have a child. He says we could have a baby girl. Then Chad would have a sister. But I do not love Alden in that way. He told me that I will grow to love him when I get well. I feel well now. Maybe I will* never be well in the way that Alden thinks I will be.

I am probably lost here in the world. Nothing feels like it did when Federico and I were together. No matter where in space I go, I do not feel like I belong. Maybe I should return to Venice. I will not kill myself. I must remember that Federico did not find me when I was dead. I tried so hard to see through the mist, to hear his voice whispering in the wind.

I need to tell you that I am very sad tonight. I am beginning to forget exactly what Federico looks like. That man on the moon ... I think he looks a little like Federico. But not his eyes. I will never forget Federico's eyes.

~ Jessica

"Mr. Lucci, that data search on Fernando Welsh is complete. I copied it off for you."

Anne Jeffries entered Walter's office and placed a four page document on his desk.

"Just four pages?"

"Yes Sir. That's it."

Several moments later Walter asked for Anne to return to his office.

"This is inadequate. These papers tell me nothing about this guy."

Walter started laughing at himself.

"Sorry Anne. This piece of information isn't worth the paper you copied it on. It looks like he had a tough childhood and didn't come from well educated parents. But that doesn't tell me anything about his character."

Walter laughed again.

"Well, maybe it would tell me something if I was a psychiatrist. But seeing that I am not, could you please get Howard McClarren on the screen. He's head of Zandia Excavating. Try him at his lunar office. Thanks Anne."

Five minutes later Howard McClarren appeared on the screen.

"Yes Walter! Good to see you. When are we going to have dinner up here again?"

"Hopefully, very soon Howard. My son and grandson are up there now. They are over at the Galaxy."

"That is our finest resort, by far, Walt. Get up here and I'll get you the best suite at the Galaxy and we'll take a walk outside!"

"We'll do it, Howard. I asked Anne to signal you up so I could get some information about a man who works for Zandia. He has been stationed at crater Italiano for several years. His name is Fernando Welsh. He is 41 years old,

American born and a Lunar Tech grad from Arizona. I got a few pages from Data-Search. I want to know what kind of man he is, not a bunch of damn clinical washed stats."

"I'm looking at his record at Zandia. It looks like he has a good work ethic going for him, Walt. He un-mooned some artifacts when he first came here. It looks like he dug up an acrylic case with remains of an old Earth sea vessel in it. That was some months back. Now as I recall Walt, it has been rumored around here for years that you buried something out in crater Italiano over ten years ago. Could that be it by any chance?" Howard grinned.

"Now Howard, speaking of a man's character, do you think a man of your splendid reputation should be listening to gossipy rumors?"

When their laughter was spent, Howard closed the conversation with a promise to discover specifically what the character of Fernando Welsh, LTE was known to be among his co-workers.

"Anne, you're joking. Fernando Welsh is here? This is too much of a coincidence. Send him in."

Fernando's penetrating brown eyes startled Walter. There was no time for Walter to remove the photo from his desk, the photo of Jessica and Chad, signed, 'Here we are on the moon. With our love, Jessica and Chad'.

"Young man, I will be direct. As I told you during our brief video phone conversation, for me to tell you anything further, I need to know more about you. Do you know who I am? Who I was?"

Fernando was staring at the photo of Jessica.

"Yes Sir, I do. You were Armister De Angelo and my name was Federico Fernando De Silva."

Walter was paled.

"Please leave right now."

Walter walked out of his office. Anne bristled in to escort Fernando Welsh to the descending tube ride to the streets of New York City.

The 'Gentlemen's Lounge' at the Berlshire Hotel was a private club. The ambiance was old world nautical. Rare oak paneling covered the floor and walls. Portal windows from the salvage of the 'Queen Mary I' looked out from the lounge to the skyline of the great city of New York.

Walter Lucci and Turner Olson, Esquire stood at one of the large portal windows and raised their glasses.

"Here's to ... The Big Apple!"

"Hey Walt, do you think there is anyone here under fifty that would have a clue about what we just toasted to?"

Walter's smile once again defied all rumors that life was not worth living.

"Yes, Turner my man, we might be getting old!"

Walter seated himself at a small oak table, wincing as he remembered the day's events at his office.

"I am here tonight with you Turner, to exclaim my gratitude to the Almighty! We as a people in the world have lost many civil rights as the years progressed. But thank God, we have not lost our right to confidential counsel by attorney."

Turner Olson filled their glasses from the bottle of merlot wine.

"So you can tell by now, Turner, I need to tell you about an experience that I am having that puts every space trip I ever took, right under the table. I have re-membered my life in the late 1800's, remembered a Miss Jessica Goodwin and her lover Federico De Silva. My role was Armister, first mate to De Silva and husband of Olivia. A very fine woman I might add."

Walter sighed heavily. A strange feeling of relief swept over him.

"First, I must tell you that this story came to my memory in bits and pieces. Like love all draped in mel-ody and shining in colors that transcend Earth. I know this sounds crazy Turner, but I believe that time has col-lapsed for me and yet life goes on."

Walter and Turner exited the tube at the Berlshire Hotel and stepped into private escort.

"It doesn't take ... It doesn't take long for me to see ... um ... what needs to be done now Walter."

When Turner Olson was trying to make a profound point he had a way of expressing himself in drawn out, lengthy syllables. On this occasion Walter was barely tolerating the slow speed in which Turner was delivering his assessment.

"I think we should approach Charles Warren. Explain that a record wiping of Jessica's identity needs to take place. And of course we will assure him that the Federal Securities of Information will approve the measure, due to her vulnerability and the possible compromise of her safety."

Walter was wishing he had not had that second glass of wine.

"So, I screwed up that bad Turner?"

Turner Olson picked up the pace of his verbiage with hyper-speed and spelled it all out.

"This character Welsh is probably a gigolo, to borrow an old term. He's not a low IQ guy. He has obviously found a way to retrieve Jessica's medical record. The psychiatric notes would explain his awareness of your part in the story. The only missing piece is how he connected the bottled ship to Jessica Englund Warren. He would have to be quite a researcher. He must be … a devil of a researcher. We must make sure that he doesn't find her. But, Walter, today, unless you get a Federal record wipe and take on a new ID, any half brained con can get all the info on her that they want. It's just part of the 21st century. It is a snap to pull up all the names and addresses of travelers to the moon. You can read them back to 1960 something. And a flight that took place from Earth to the moon this week! Get the idea Walt? I'll begin the Federal appeal for a wipe of ID tonight."

Walter exited the private escort at his apartment building. Giant flakes of snow paused on his overcoat before melting. He looked back at Turner Olson and nodded.

Charles Warren was planted firmly in front of the blazing fireplace in his study. Beads of perspiration stung his eyes before they slid down his face and landed on the lapel of his vest. Lauren had opened the foyer to Walter Lucci and his attorney Turner Olson.

"Walter, I just cannot believe what you are telling me. There is a man named Fernando Welsh looking for Jessica? Our Jessica!"

Lauren felt a sudden flushing tingle.

Turner Olson rose to his feet.

"Mr. and Mrs. Warren, we do not know how this fellow Welsh has become interested in finding your daughter. But he did come to Walter's office with a wild story about thinking he was Federico De Silva. He has surely gained access to her medical records. This is very unfortunate of course. But if you will agree as Jessica's legal guardians, I assure you and Mrs. Warren that we will get Federal Securities approval and all of her identity records will be erased. Time is of the essence. I am presuming that Jessica's current address here at Skyscape Towers can be found in her medical record at Joseph Murphy Healing Center on Long Island?"

"Of course it is! Bring me that weasel and I will personally break every bone in his body!"

"Although Fernando Welsh hasn't broken any laws as of yet, Mr. Warren, Walter did contact me yesterday with his concerns. Those concerns are legitimate. Jessica shall receive a new identity within days."

"A new identity!"

Charles was livid.

"Oh! As if my daughter doesn't have identity issues *now*!"

"As Walter explained the delicate situation to me, it became clear that Jessica does not need to know that her identity has been legally changed to another name at this time. Well...not for a while at least. She doesn't move about the city unescorted I take it? And besides, if she should use her former name, there will be no record of it. We will recommend that her first given name remain. The last name must be changed. The Federal Security Board will choose the new last name. That is the protocol."

Charles reached for his pen to sign the prepared document. His hands were shaking uncontrollably.

"Walter, so help me! If this isn't the best thing to do, I will never let you near Jessi again!"

Lauren rose to her feet. "Charles, you must apologize to Walter this minute."

"I will apologize to Walter Lucci when I am convinced that this will not hurt Jessi more than she has already been hurt."

# GLASS BOTTLES

The silence in Charles' study was deafening. There was no crackling sound of the burning wood. Shadowy flames ominously reflected across their faces. Walter said a silent prayer, grateful that the mention of Armister had not been necessary. He and Turner rose to leave.

⌣⌐

Lauren felt a twang of paranoia as she stepped with Jessi from private escort into 'Le Shoppe', a fine Fifth Avenue boutique.

"Look Lauren, this dress is very lovely."

Lauren followed Jessi to a mannequin adorned with a dress that flowed with a long sweeping skirt and bustier camisole trimmed with cream colored lace.

"Oh, it is lovely, Jessi. So ... so retro! And the more I look at it, the more I can't help but think how really hot Alden would think this dress is."

Lauren found herself blushing.

"Oh Jessi, I don't know what made me say that. It was not an appropriate thing for your mother to say to you! Whatever has gotten into me? I have no clue!"

"Lauren, are you worried about me?"

"Jessica, you have always been so very perceptive. I'm really embarrassed. I really am. Yes, I have been thinking that you would ... would ... be safer somehow... if you married Alden."

*January 13th, 2052*

*Dear Diary,*

*Lauren is so dear to me. She and Charles have looked at me with such tenderness of late.*

*Walter has signaled me on the phone every day since I returned from the moon. I love him so much.*

*I think they want me to marry Alden.*
*For some strange reason they do not know that Federico will find me soon. They all say that I cannot go to Venice now. That is not alright with me. I love them all, especially Chad, but I need to go to Venice, so that Federico will find me.*

*I have seen that I cannot just get on a steamer bound for Venice. I have seen that if I flew shuttle it might be acceptable. I could fly there.*

*Lauren and Charles will forgive me when I signal them up and tell them that I am very fine in Venice.*

*I will bring Federico back to the United States with me. Yes. That is what I will do. He will understand. He always understands. Everyone here in New York will love him as I do.*

*~ Jessica*


"I would like to purchase fare to Venice, Italy."

"We do not have a direct flight to Venice. Please dial EarthLines. That number is 812-798-471-8882."

Jessi dialed for EarthLines.

"Reservations division. This is EarthLines. How may I help you?"

The woman on the phone seemed pleasant, but did not appear on the screen.

"Oh yes. One ticket to Italy. To Venice, Italy, please."

"Your name?"

"Jessica Englund Warren."

"One moment."

Jessi felt her heart pounding.

"I do not find a Warren, Jessica Englund, listed for having approved passport for destination ... Venice Italy."

"Oh, but I have my passport right here in my hand."

"Please read me the US number on the upper right hand side of your passport."

"90K-77-B342-907."

"I am sorry, that does not compute. Thank you for calling EarthLines."

With the quick disconnect, Jessi was suddenly aware of the fact that she had been speaking to a 'pleasant' computer.

Jessi smiled to herself and said aloud,

"I will ask Chad how to arrange my trip to Venice."


"Jessi, maybe you need a new computer. I can't pull your name up for passports and when I do a broad search, nothing comes up in your name."

"Oh Chad. I just haven't learned about computers yet."

"Let's see. It's an old '38 processor. It runs on a wireless modem, but it should pull up records anyway. Do you have a data-stat program in here?"

"A data-stat program?"

"Yeah, its software made for these old models. You buy the program and get a key to stick into the processor. It's like an app Jessi. But more downloads needed to be done."

Chad leaned under Jessi's desk and lifted the small tower.

"Nope. But this is way rad. You have a LUNA real-time video program in here!"

Chad set the browser, and he and Jessi were off to the moon ... again. After a small channel adjustment the two were soon watching a closed circuit meeting of a group of men. The group was seated at a table in what appeared to be a business office with the lunar landscape visible from the observation area.

"Jessi, this is clearer than the feed from my LUNA III program! Here, I'm gonna zoom in and let's listen to the audio."

"Chad, let's not."

Jessi stopped in mid-sentence as the camera spanned the room. The man seated at the end of table was, unmistakably, John Bayer of Zandia Excavating. Jessi watched the screen in quiet amazement. The meeting appeared to be ending. The man seated at the head of the table stood and dismissed the group. With business attended to, the man motioned to John Bayer to remain for a moment. Jessi could now see the insignia on the officer's uniform. It read 'Howard McClarren COZE'.

Jessi broke her silence.

"Chad, they don't know we are watching them. Let's stop now."

"Oh Jessi. Just a minute longer. Please?"

The two men saluted, and Howard McClarren handed John Bayer a computerized disc.

"Play this chip, Bayer. Record me your findings. I want to know everything about this guy. This is on the QT."

John saluted and left the office.

"Wow Jessi! There can't be anything wrong with this old computer. I'll try to find your passport on my computer when I get home."

Jessi was left staring at the empty office on the moon.

⌒

Fernando Welsh had been back with his lunar crew for a month and was aware of John Bayer's recent change in attitude. One evening in January, seated at the bar of the Galaxy Resort lounge, Nando downed a shot of whiskey and turned to John.

"What if I was to tell you that before I left Earth last month I found out that Jessica is alive?"

"Nah. She doesn't exist, man."

"I know she does, John. You don't happen to know why you missed seeing her here at The Galaxy do you? When I video phoned you December 9th, you were right here. This is where she stayed, John. The records are clear as they can be. She was right here in this dome! You still expect me to believe that you didn't see her?"

"You're sick, man. You sound threatening. Get a grip on the cortex of your small brain. And drop this crap. If you are so sure that she exists, then tell me this. Where is she, Nando?"

Fernando was on his feet. The bartender reached for the security alarm.

"Gentlemen, do I need to press this red signal button?"

Both men immediately deescalated. They knew their jobs were on the line if they did not contain themselves. Nando left the bar, knowing he would be denied another shot of whiskey.

John Bayer re-read his report before converting the content to microchip.

"Attention: Captain McClarren:

The person of interest appears to be emotionally disturbed. As a party chief, his work is acceptable. He prepares his crew's assignment at the beginning of each exit period. We know what is expected of us. All correct equipment is issued to the crew. Safety is of paramount importance. I have never felt in physical danger with him as my party chief.

Away from the job site he has become insistent that a woman exists, from one of his past lives. I apologize for the bizarre nature of this part of my report. I thought at first that his fantasies were based on a ship in a bottle that he found on crater Italiano several months ago. It has become well known that retired General Walter Lucci buried the remains of an 1800's schooner model at crater 'Italiano', over a decade ago.

This evening I met with the person of interest. He became quite agitated. He insisted that I knew this woman from the 1800's. He insisted that I had lied to him. Signed... John Austin Bayer LT"

Fernando Welsh was terminated from Zandia Excavating one week later. His return flight to Earth ended at the US Air Force Base, south of Colorado Springs, Colorado. The termination documents were stamped 'Medical-Confidential'. There were four years' severance pay provided, and medical benefits for life.

⌒

"Dad, how come Jessi isn't on line anywhere and isn't on 'data-stat', or even 'credi-stat'?"

"Chad, have you entered 'Jessica Englund Warren?'"

"I did. I've checked the code key and ran a bug check on all my programs. I can pull up any other of our names on six apps!"

"Why are you searching for Jessi?"

Chad turned to leave the room and called back to Alden. "Oh, it's nothing, Dad. I've been trying to help her learn about apps and programs."

Alden touched his screen to 'data-stat' app and began a search of Jessica Englund Warren. The first failed attempt to retrieve any data was of no concern. After several repeated attempts with different search engines, it was clear that someone had wiped her electronic records from the internet. Alden signaled Walter on video phone.

"Pops, something strange is going on with Jessi's ID records. All ID data searches come up empty. Do you know if the Warren's had her records Fed-wiped?"

Walter remained quiet for a moment.

"Can't discuss this on the phone. I'll meet you for dinner at 'The Berlshire' at 18:00 hours."


Lauren walked passed Jessi's room and noticed her sitting quietly in front of the monitor. Chad had left the LUNA live feed program up and running on her pc before leaving the apartment.

"Jessi, we could get some shopping done today if you'd like to join me." Jessi aimlessly pressed a few keys on her keyboard.

"Are you alright, Jessi?"

"Yes Mom, I just don't remember how to shut off the computer."

Lauren was stunned to hear Jessi call her 'Mom'. Fighting back a display of emotions, she pulled up a chair next to Jessi at the desk.

"We don't need to go shopping today Jessi. Here, let me show you some things about your computer. These are the files. In these folders are things you saved. You used this computer for several years before you became ill. Here is the list of titled files. Do you want to open one?"

"Yes, please open one."

"You pick which one, Jessi. Just touch the screen here. These are your private files so I'll go downstairs and you call me on intercom when you are ready and I'll come back up and show you whatever you want to know about the computer."

"File - 'My Documents' title: 'research' - De Silva, Federico Fernando ... born 1855 ... Rome Italy ..." Jessi continued to read in amazement. "... shipping companies ... no record of marriage ... no date of death ..."

Jessi opened a file titled 'Personal': 'text e-mail saved'.

"To: jessibird@timeless.insta
From: aldenlucci@pcmasters.now
Received: 23:21, 03-13-44
Hi Jessi Bird! Mom and Pops want you, Chad, and me ... to get our medium, little, and large butts (in that order) over to their place for dinner Sunday. So if it's OK with you I won't bring Chad over Sunday morning but will wait until 15:00 and we'll pick you up. Alden"

"To: jessibird@timeless.insta
From: kaylynduncan7B@ultranow.stat
Received: 21:40, 03-17-44

"Jessi, I just read your article on Claude Monet. It is off the page fabulous. The prints of his parasol ladies that you used in your article have given me a great idea for our new French countryside web-page. Do I have to get permission from Timeless magazine? I hope not. Let me know. I would like to use three of your prints. Your bud forever ~ KD"

Jessi read on for pages. She read file after file. On into the January night, she read. And while she read, she pondered.

*January 15th, 2052*

*Dear Diary,*

*My hands are shaking as I write this. I have seen what happened to me. Something happened to my brain.*

*I think it must have been a very bad accident. I was writing articles for Timeless Magazine when it happened.*

*I had a beautiful apartment here in Manhattan. Chad was very young at the time.*

*I remember now.*

When I became conscious, I was dreaming about a man who owned the schooner 'Liberty'. I had been researching this man, Federico De Silva, since I found a model of his 1800's schooner at a nautical shop at the harbor.

When I had the accident, I think I was depressed. I remember Mom yelling my name and crying. I couldn't move or speak. It felt like I was floating by the ceiling and watching our bodies in my apartment.

Thank you for helping me dear diary. I think I am well now. I am going downstairs and tell Mom and Dad that I woke up.

~Jessica

Walter Lucci lifted his hand for the waiter. The members-only dining room at the Berlshire Hotel was unusually quiet.

"Please carry my tab into the lounge."

Walter and Alden stood. During dinner Walt had acknowledged that the Warren's had Jessica's identity federally wiped from the internet. He had not given details. There was a sway in his gait as he and Alden entered the lounge. Alden guided his Pops towards a table by a nautical portal window.

"Dad, let's go home."

"You're right, son. I am going to have to get very drunk if you are ever going to hear the whole story."

The two descended the tube and in minutes arrived, by personal escort, at Marge and Walter's apartment.

"Thank goodness your mother has gone upstate with your Aunt Viv. Son, I am going to fill this snifter with a fine cognac, light a real wood fire in that fireplace and tell you the whole damn story. But please never tell your mother. I think she would leave me if she knew how bad I screwed things up."

Alden poured himself a brandy and sunk into the overstuffed recliner in his father's study. The fire was blazing quickly. Walter spoke.

"I let a lying con artist hacker by the name of Fernando Welsh into my office and acknowledged that Jessica was alive. A few days after the Feds agreed that Jessi might be in danger, another man, even more of a con, some guy named John Bayer, phoned me from the moon asking about Jessica. Both low lives are looking for new jobs. I am so disgusted with myself. Just the thought that I got caught up in Jessica's fantasy, Son, I can't tell you how horrible I feel."

Walter took a deep gulp from the snifter and reached out again … for the glass bottle of cognac.

# FIVE

Many citizens of the Phoenix metropolitan area had moved to outlying suburbs. The suburbs boasted of giant shopping centers and subdivisions with climate control domes covering homes, schools and office buildings. All legal vehicles were solar or hydro electric powered. The Arizona landscape bore a striking resemblance to the lunar colonies.

Justin Welsh was working as a paramedic for Emerg-Care, an ambulance company that served the old urban area of Phoenix. He slipped his access card into the door of Fernando's rented apartment on the south side of Phoenix. The stench of rotting food was overwhelming.

"Bro?"

Justin walked through the modest living room after entering his palm print onto the scanner. It was obvious that the apartment had not been opened to fresh air in months. The manual force required to open the window triggered an ear blasting alarm. Indoor security lights instantly activated and a recorded voice boomed through the intercom system.

"Police authorities are en route to this property. A signal of illegal entry has been received."

The alarm system was becoming deafening. Justin jumped back as Fernando touched his shoulder.

"How do we shut this thing off?"

Nando was holding a satellite phone to one ear while his finger remained firmly plugged in the other. It was impossible to hear spoken words. Justin covered his ears, ran to the front entry and stopped in the fourth story corridor of the building. Several doors were ajar as people gingerly peeked out into the hallway, their ring-bolt door locks remaining firmly in place. After what seemed like a lifetime, the alarm was silenced and Justin slowly closed the door to Nando's apartment.

Nando had begun running the garbage disposal and was compacting food containers for release into the sanitary refuse shoot. The odor was being cleared from the room, so despite the ear trauma, Justin's window opening had been an effective maneuver.

"Your thoughts are all in line with the facts, Justin. You are right on about my lazy approach to this life that I'm supposed to be living. My Zandia severance pay is nearly spent. I drink way too much. But ya know the worst part? Don't answer that. I know what you are thinking and you are correct. I am no closer to filling this deep hole in me than I was when you and I were doing search and rescue in Washington State."

Justin eased into an old bulky lounge chair from the 2020's. He had nothing to say.

"Wanna beer, Jus?'

"No, I'll pass for now. I have to be at work in about an hour, providing that my damn ear drums aren't ruptured, Nando. Anyway, I came over to show you my new transportation machine man. Wanna come down to the parking lot and take a spin in it?"

"Better not, Bro. Had a few drinks before you came over. What wheels did you buy?"

Fernando reached for a glass bottle of beer.

"She's a real prize Nando. A Delbe 140 with wheel spoke rims right out of 2010. The design of the car is as retro as the antique turbo Stallions of the 2030's. Ya gotta take it for a run. Let's put it on the old NASCAR track this weekend and I'll show you a gut grabbing ride!"

"Ok Justin. I'll make a point to be sober and I'll spend the day with you and your screaming machine. How are your ears by the way?"

"They've been better, thanks Nando."

Fernando's head had dropped toward his chest and a soft snoring sound filled the living room. Justin rose from the old chair that must have cradled hundreds of bodies in its day, and quietly left the apartment. He didn't notice the tear on Nando's face as it silently rolled down his cheek and dripped to his shirt.

⌒

Walter Lucci woke himself up thrashing amongst the bed covers that were drenched with his sweat. It was 4:00 am. Walter's wife Marge was standing by the bedside.

"Wake up, Walter. You are having a terrible dream."

She reached for the room climate control remote and, after checking the temperature, pressed to raise the room lighting to resemble early dawn. Walter sat up in bed as Marge handed him a towel to dry his face.

"Oh dear God Marge. I had a ... I saw ... Oh my God! I heard Federico De Silva as clearly as I hear you right now. It was in a storm of rain and pounding surf on the rocks. He was trying desperately to bring the ship home. Oh so dark and cold. I'm soaking wet and freezing."

"Here Walter, you change your night clothes and I'll get dry bed linens right now."

Walter managed to follow Marge's instruction and though still shaking, seated himself in a soft high-back chair in their master bedroom. He sipped tea from an oversized mug.

"Walter who is Federico De Silva?"

"Fernando Welsh."

"And who is Fernando Welsh?"

"I'm going to the living room and start a log in the fireplace Marge. I'm chilled to the bone. You try to get more rest. It was all just a bad, a very bad dream."

The following morning, February 3, 2056, Walter Lucci did not go to his office. Marge was deeply concerned about his agitation following the previous night's dream. She was an assertive woman and after bringing a sandwich and cup of soup to Walter's library desk at midday, she plunked her small frame into a chair near his desk and spoke directly.

"Walter who is Fernando Welsh? The intensity of your reaction to the dream, nightmare, whatever ... was physiologically dangerous for your heart condition. I insist that you speak to me about this episode. "

Walter sunk deeper into his high-back desk chair.

"It has to with Jessica Warren, who now has a new last name that I am not privy to know."

"Jessica? What possibly could our dear Jessica do to upset you to this degree? That is preposterous, Walter. And what do you mean that Warren is no longer her last name. Oh, don't tell me that she and our Alden have secretly married and you didn't tell me!"

Marge was on her feet.

"No Marge. It isn't like what you just said, but I am responsible for the fact that Jessi has had her identity records federally wiped off the map, literally and figuratively."

"And Walter, how and why did that happen?"

The scowl on Marge's forehead etched canyon deep lines across her usually serene appearance.

"I messed up very badly and I need to get in touch with Fernando Welsh immediately."

"Again Walter, who is Fernando Welsh?"

"Jessi's soul mate, Marge. He is Jessi's soul mate."

⌣

"Go easy, Bro. Ease into that solar-power real gently when you ignite the start connection or we are going to fly through this parking area and hit some building before we know it happened."

Justin's face was beaming pride as Fernando eased into the driver's seat.

"A slight touch. Use a real light touch, Bro."

With lightning speed Justin's trans-solar-auto, with Nando in the driver's seat, peeled from the apartment parking area and sped toward the privately owned NASCAR track on the west side of Phoenix.

"Justin, you gotta' tell me how to slow this baby down or we are gonna have serious damage happenin'."

Justin was laughing. His only comment was lost in the propulsion of the acceleration.

"Nando, you gotta' lean into this experience like a captain."

Fernando squinted in the sunlight, and then pressed the control on his helmet for diffusion of UV rays.

"What a ride Justin. Thank you, Bro. What a ride."

Marge broke the silence.

"Walter, I was out of line this morning. I think you need to do whatever you must do to come to peace within yourself, no matter how upset you are right now. It obviously was not ever your intention to include me in this ... this ... whatever it was that happened with Jessi. If our son Alden is involved, then all I have to say to you this moment, is you two better get this straightened out right now!"

Marge exited the library, blinking away tears that just kept falling. Walter called out back to his wife.

"The thing is, Marge, Alden has nothing to do with this. Well, at least not directly."

But Marge was out of ear shot.

"Anne, please come in my office."

Walter sat behind his desk and stared out of his Manhattan office window. The years of Walter's service to the lunar projects had elevated him to a comfortable and respected public status, plus a generous pension for life. The office was spacious and the interior was artfully designed with magnificently framed NASA photos of the lunar surface. 1960's Gemini mission photos were among the art collection, and numerous Apollo mission artifacts included a glass contained display of moon rocks and other space memorabilia.

Anne Jeffries stepped into Walter's office.

"Anne, please get me Howard McClarren of Zandia Excavating on satellite screen."

Within moments Howard's face appeared on the screen.

"Walter, my man! You haven't taken me up on my offer of the Galaxy Resort accommodations and I feel that if this call up from you is about that issue, I will be one delighted man."

"Hey Howard. Yes, Marge looks like she might need a holiday and I intend to book us soon."

"Well, you'd better let me take care of the whole trip, Walter. I won't settle for less. It will be first class all the way and you'll make me a most honored man."

"I thank you, friend. I thank you. I've got a problem going on though. It's a problem that I need to approach differently than I did a few years back. It's the Fernando Welsh issue, Howard. The Zandia employee that you investigated for me."

"What's going on with that, Walt?"

"Well, I'm having a difficult time coming to resolution about setting him up for dismissal from Zandia. There have been further developments."

Walter paused.

"Take your time Walt. I'm right here, and there is no place I'd rather be than speaking with you right now."

"Well, I guess I need to start with the report, the one of John Bayer's regarding Fernando Welsh's performance as a party chief. And his view of this man's mental health status."

"Did you replay the report and hear something that we missed when we listened to it together?"

"No, Howard. It's not quite like that. In recent days I have come to see that John Bayer met Jessica Warren at the Galaxy Resort, in the bar, and knew who she was. He knew that she was the woman that Fernando Welsh was looking for."

"It's alright Walt. You don't need to tell me more. How can I help?"

After what felt to be the passing of a lifetime, Walter managed to resume speaking.

"Thank you, Howard. I just need the address where Zandia sent Fernando Welsh's severance pay installments or the name of the bank if the payments were direct deposits."

"You'll have it in one minute, Walt. And I expect to see you and Marge up here within the next few months. Hear me Walt?"

"That's a deal, my friend. That is a deal."

Fernando Welsh eased his stressed body into the lumpy green lounge chair. Although still a little shaken by the vibration from the virtual speed attained on the NASCAR track, he was feeling somewhat uplifted by the experience. He reached out to pour another drink... but the glass bottle was empty. Fumbling a bit, Nando opened his satellite phone. Justin's face appeared on the screen.

"Hey Nando. Are you OK?"

"No. Can you come over? Like, now?"

By the time Justin's wheels screeched into the street, Fernando was feeling slightly more put together. His brother found him sitting on the floor, stuffing clothes into a large sports bag.

"I have to leave here tonight."

"Whoa Nando, are you sure about this?"

"I've never been so sure about anything. There is more to my life than this. I've wasted so much time. Jessica is real. She isn't a figment of my imagination."

Justin could see that Nando's decision had been made. He shook his head as he listened to yet another version of his brother's distress.

"OK. You go have a shower. I'll drop you off at the Trans Terminal. It's late, but you're sure to pick up a ride going west...but wait a minute...where are you going?"

As cold water from the shower ran over his face and down his body, Fernando shivered.

The phone signaled, and with a jerk of his head that sent water spraying in all directions from his thick, black hair, he called out.

"Did you get that call, Justin?"

"It's some guy. He says his name is Walter Lucci."

"Disconnect the phone, Justin.   Disconnect the bastard."

On the way to the terminal Fernando clutched the prepaid Cash-Card that Justin had pressed into his hand. At his feet rested a bag.  Inside, was an acrylic case, holding the remains of the schooner model 'Liberty'.  There was no more to be said.  Justin glanced in the rear view mirror at his brother standing alone in moonlight.

After making his way along the pier Fernando closed his eyes and inhaled the salty sea air.  The smell of sea soaked wooden pylons and the screeching of gulls filled his senses with nostalgia.  Wiping the first drops of rain from his face he turned toward the heavy clouds rolling in from the east.  The sudden darkening of the sky sent shivers to his soul.  Everything in his awareness was being swallowed into the approaching darkness.  The haloed lights at the entrance to the pier dimmed from view.  Pylons moved and creaked beneath him as the waves became stronger.  The noise of the sea mingled with the howling wind. Covering his ears, Fernando could not block the ear splitting crack of the impact as his memory of the schooner Liberty rushed back into awareness. The schooner was flung with raging force against the rocks, in to screams of splintering wood. Jessica was dead. All attempts to bring the best physician to her side had failed Federico De Silva.

With one smooth movement of Fernando's arm, the model of 'Liberty My Jessica' was flung into the stormy Atlantic Ocean.

"Sleep, silent Angel. Not only I am present, but so must you be… Jessica. No matter where you are in time, you are as alive as I am."

Fernando Welsh walked back towards the lights of New York City, drenched in rain … and memory.


"Jessi your apartment is lovely. It's so lovely!"

It was December 4th, 2056. Kaylyn had purchased two tickets to see the premiere Broadway play of 'Born to Love'. She placed the tickets on the table alongside the latest issue of 'Timeless' magazine.

"Your new article was brilliant. It must be wonderful to be back at work."

"Thanks Kaylyn, it is good. Let's get going. Private escort will be slow tonight."

The two women exited the main door of Kent Tower apartments and dashed out through the light rain. Just as the chauffeur opened the door of the waiting escort and

Kaylyn slid inside, a man stepped across the sidewalk and touched Jessi's arm.

"Jessica?"

Kaylyn pulled Jessi into the vehicle.

"Jessi, you are doing so well, but don't ever let any stranger touch you."

Jessica settled into the plush seat.

"But... Kaylyn! Did you see his eyes?"

**~ The End ~**

# AUTHOR BIOGRAPHY

J L Goodwin practiced psychiatric nursing as a registered nurse for fifteen years. She has published her first novella. Glass Bottles is one of her stories. She holds a Ph.D. in metaphysics and continues to study world religions and cultural philosophy. With a background in astrology and fine arts, this author finds the gift of today, yesterday, and tomorrow, richly intrinsic.

www.ingramcontent.com/pod-product-compliance
Lightning Source LLC
Chambersburg PA
CBHW060628130626
46555CB00002B/704